A SEAL's Seduction

AN ALPHA SEALS NOVEL

Makenna Jameison

ISBN: 9781717946379

ALSO BY MAKENNA JAMEISON

ALPHA SEALS

SEAL the Deal
SEALED with a Kiss
A SEAL's Surrender
A SEAL's Seduction
The SEAL Next Door
Protected by a SEAL
Loved by a SEAL
Tempted by a SEAL
Married to a SEAL
Seduced by a SEAL
Rescued by a SEAL
Stranded with a SEAL
Summer with a SEAL
Kidnapped by a SEAL
SEAL Ever After

Table of Contents

Chapter 1

Mike "Patch" Hunter locked and loaded his HK416 assault rifle, taking aim at the target downrange. There was a slight breeze on the brisk autumn day, whispering across his skin, and he adjusted his calculations accordingly. It was cool out. Clear. His finger itched as he caressed the trigger, ready to take the shot. Guaranteed to meet his mark. The target sat immobile 200 yards from where he stood, not exactly the same as the fast-moving targets his SEAL team took out in battle. But hell, he'd taken plenty of kill shots to unaware men. Drug kingpins. Terrorists. Armed guards. All part of his duty to Uncle Sam and the US Navy.

Just this spring his SEAL team had been sent on an op to the Middle East to retrieve a high-value asset. The other guys had been on the ground ready to grab him. Mike had the sniper's roost across the street, and when their target—needed captured not

1

killed—stepped out of the building flanked by two bodyguards, he'd taken them out in an instant. Pow. Pow. They hadn't even known what had hit them.

Mike spat on the ground beside his dusty boots before returning his eyes to the prize. The men around him fired off shots on the range, and a couple of his SEAL buddies stood behind him, watching, but he tuned everything out. Let his vision tunnel. The only thing that existed was the target.

The slight chill in the air nipped at his skin. He blinked. Focused. It was nothing but him and his weapon. In the zone.

Eye on the scope, he pulled the trigger.

Bullseye.

Every damn time.

"Not bad, man," his fellow team member Christopher "Blade" Walters said as Mike pulled off his headset and glanced back. Christopher lounged beside Brent "Cobra" Rollins, both of them looking relaxed and ready to roll onto the next part of their Saturday.

Despite their intense training at Naval Amphibious Base Little Creek Monday through Friday, the three of them had headed to a local gun range today to get in some practice and unwind. Or something like that. What was it about weapons and fresh air that made a man so damn content? The adrenaline rush of his job was what kept Mike going half the time, ready to take on the whole world. And shooting on the weekend with his buddies? He was fired up and ready to go, energy surging through his veins.

"Not bad?" Mike laughed. "That was fucking spectacular."

Brent raised his eyebrows. "Modest as always,

asshole."

"I get it," Mike said. "You're jealous of my good looks, talent, and way with the ladies."

Brent guffawed. "Not a chance in hell."

Mike held back a grin. While some of the guys on their SEAL team were content playing happily-ever-after with their women, Mike, Brent, and the third single guy on their team, Matthew "Gator" Murphy, still enjoyed carousing for ladies at the local bar. Although Mike enjoyed female company when the mood struck, he usually kept things light. The chase was part of the fun, and some of those girls that hung around him and the other guys were just too damn easy to be caught.

While Mike and Matthew had enjoyed their fair share of women over the years—hell, maybe *more* than their fair share—no one seemed to have more fun than Brent. A new woman every night was his MO, and the trail of broken hearts in his wake was a mile long. At least.

"Speaking of the ladies," Christopher interrupted as he stood. "I told Lexi I'd be back soon. Are you about wrapped up here or do I have to hoof it back to my apartment?"

Mike chuffed out a laugh. That guy was whipped. "Is she bringing any of her friends to the party tonight?" he nonchalantly asked as he gathered his gear.

Christopher's gaze flicked over to him as Brent's ears perked up. "Kenley will be there, if that's what you're asking."

"Hell."

Brent guffawed. "She's still pissed at you?"

"Something like that," Mike muttered.

The petite, brunette beauty with a head full of curls and angelic face was a friend of Lexi's. Lexi and Christopher were old flames who had rekindled their love over the summer after a chance encounter. Lexi, an IT whiz, had been sent down to their base in Little Creek from the Pentagon to stop some attempted hackings to their secure networks.

When she was kidnapped by the man behind the ploy, her best friend Kenley had come racing to Virginia Beach to help find her. As Mike and Christopher had searched the condo Lexi had been in the afternoon she went missing, Kenley had appeared from one of the bedrooms. Mistaking her for an intruder, Mike had instantly pinned her to the wall. And holy hell.

Trapping her small, curvy frame against his had made him harder than steel.

At that moment, he hadn't even cared if she was the enemy or not. He'd had a sample, and he needed more.

Her soft breasts had pressed against his hard chest, her lips almost brushing against his neck as he held her in place, her soft breath whispering against his skin. His fingers had wound round both of her slender wrists, holding her immobile, and the vanilla scent she wore had permeated the room, making his mind fuzzy and his dick stand at attention.

The second he'd realized she was Lexi's friend, not a foe, he'd been a goner. He had images of holding her body against the wall every night as he drilled into her, sinking his throbbing cock into her soft, wet heat as she whimpered for more. As he pleasured her again and again. No doubt a woman as gorgeous as her was used to a man's attention, but hell if he wouldn't love to be the one to have the honor of exploring every one of her curves—and then making her come in every way imaginable.

She was so small, he could easily hold her up as he took her, lifting her petite body up and down his shaft. Her legs would wrap round his waist, and she'd arch back in ecstasy as he made her come in his arms.

On his cock.

He wondered if she tasted of vanilla or something else sinfully sweet. If she'd been wet as he held her there against his hard body—God knows he'd been thick and throbbing for her the second he'd touched her.

Not that she'd exactly seen it the same way.

She'd trembled for him, but from fear, not arousal. Christopher had growled at him to get off of her, and the split second he'd realized she was Lexi's friend, he'd gone from aggressor to protector. He'd wanted to haul her against him again, but this time, to keep her safe from the evils that were out there. From the men who'd kidnapped her best friend.

Something didn't sit right with him at leaving her alone and defenseless in her condo while he and Christopher continued their search for Lexi, but what choice had they had? Kenley was a grown woman; she wasn't his. If she wanted to stay there, they sure the hell couldn't stop her. And Lexi had been the one being held by a crazed kidnapper, the one who needed their help.

The memories washed over him as Brent smirked. "Time to make a move, lover boy. Send her flowers or some shit like that."

Mike raised his eyebrows. Brent had never bought a woman flowers in his life. He'd probably never taken a woman out on an actual date—his bed seemed to work just fine.

"She's still pissed as hell at you from what Lexi says," Christopher said, falling in step beside them as they walked off the range. "She didn't take you pinning her against the wall like some criminal too well."

"Don't I know it," Mike admitted.

"She asked about you though," Christopher added.

Mike swung his gaze over to his friend. The way his heart pounded in his chest like a damn freight train was annoying. So what if she asked about him. Didn't mean a fucking thing.

"I think she was hoping you got shipped out—without the rest of the team," Christopher laughed.

"Crash and burn, lover boy," Brent said.

"Damn it," Mike muttered. So much for making amends. She'd probably be perfectly happy never seeing him again.

"What's this chick look like anyway?" Brent asked, eyes sparking with interest.

"Don't ask," Mike and Christopher said in unison.

Hell, Mike could understand why Kenley would be mad at him. She'd trembled against the wall as his much larger body caged her in, and it sure the hell hadn't been with desire. She had to know why they'd be on her in an instant though. Everyone had been on edge the minute Lexi was taken. Kenley herself had raced down to Virginia Beach from DC in search of her best friend. It wasn't like he made a habit of grabbing defenseless women in their own homes. The condo had been the last known location Lexi had been, and when she'd appeared unexpectedly out of the bedroom, his training had kicked in instantly.

Mike and all of the guys on his SEAL team were trained to be alert and aware in all situations. To neutralize the threat, getting in and out with their asses in one piece. They worked seamlessly as one unit, and he and Christopher hadn't even needed to utter a single word to one another as they swept the condo.

The fact that Kenley had been on the receiving end of it had been unfortunate, but it's not liked he'd harmed her. Just held her in place until he could determine who she was—and desired her more strongly than he'd ever wanted a woman before. Must be that forbidden fruit thing—he shouldn't have her, so he wanted her that much more. Mike shook his head, clearing the heated images that had been burned on his brain.

The men walked out to the parking lot, stashing their gear in the back of Mike's large SUV. He slammed the trunk shut as they each climbed into the vehicle. "So Patch, what are you up to tonight?" Brent asked Mike, addressing him by his nickname. "I know Christopher's all pussy-whipped and busy with his woman."

"Sonofabitch," Christopher muttered under his breath.

Mike smirked. Despite Brent's ribbing, Christopher was happier than ever, engaged to the love of his life. If he wanted that, then awesome for him. Mike was content living alone, flirting with the pretty girls whenever he felt like it, spending the night with one every so often. He didn't mind doing the flowers and dinner song and dance some of the time as long as the woman he was with understood he wasn't after anything long term.

He really did need to talk to Kenley tonight and formally apologize. If one of his SEAL buddies was marrying Kenley's best friend, their paths would no doubt continue to cross from time-to-time. He didn't need her feeling uncomfortable around him, and if smoothing the waters between them led to anything more, well, he sure the hell wouldn't complain. Not when the memories of her lush little body pressed firmly against his filled his brain every night.

"We've got that bonfire on the beach tonight," Christopher said. "Didn't Patrick and Rebecca invite you?"

"Hell, I guess so," Brent muttered. "I need some female companionship though, not a night with you motherfuckers."

"Are you hitting up Anchors instead?" Mike asked as he started the engine.

Anchors, a popular bar in Virginia Beach, was usually packed with single military men and plenty of available women. Their team went there on the weekends, enjoying a few drinks with their buddies before taking a woman home for the night.

Their team leader Patrick "Ice" Foster and his girlfriend, Rebecca, had organized a get together on the beach tonight instead. Each single parents, they'd started dating last spring and been inseparable ever since. There'd been a brief stalking incident, when the spouse of one of Rebecca's clients had been following her, but all's well that ends well. That dude was in jail and his teammate, "Ice," who everyone thought would never date again, seemed smitten with his woman.

The couple had organized the beach bonfire tonight for the guys on the SEAL team and their dates. Mike supposed the women his teammates were dating didn't enjoy hanging around the loud, crazy pick-up joint. Not that he blamed them. If he did ever settle down, he sure the hell wouldn't be spending his weekends at Anchors. Not that he was exactly the settling down kind. Playing the field had suited him just damn fine. And with his career of frequent deployments, long days of training, and weeks or months away, that was probably for the best.

"That depends on who's going to be at this beach party," Brent said.

"Alison is bringing along some of her nurse friends from the hospital," Christopher said, smirking. Alison, a pediatric nurse, was Evan "Flip" Jenkins's girlfriend. She'd been promising to set up some of the single guys with her friends. Mike had taken one of the pretty nurses out on a date, but the way she'd thrown herself at him had been entirely unappealing. Even for a guy like him, used to having his pick of women, he enjoyed a little bit of a challenge. An easy lay wasn't exactly what he was after.

"Just steer clear of Kenley," Christopher added, his eyes sweeping toward Mike.

Mike gripped the steering wheel tighter. "How's that?" He swallowed, trying to ignore the feelings of lust and desire churning inside him at the mere mention of her name. Hell, the way the woman wound him up like that was unnerving.

"She's still madder than hell at you. Lexi only got her to agree to come by promising to keep you away from her."

"What's she still doing in town anyway?"

Kenley lived in Northern Virginia, near Lexi. After Lexi and Christopher had gotten engaged over the summer, Lexi had put in a job application to work on base here at Little Creek. She and Christopher had been together out in Coronado years ago, and if all went according to plan, they'd be working on the same naval base again before the year was up. Lexi could keep a position with the Department of Defense but live down here with Christopher. Since Little Creek's own head of network security had been arrested as part of the hacking scandal, a position was open. With her connections and computer expertise, she'd probably be a shoo-in.

That didn't explain why Kenley had stuck around all this time. He'd seen her once since their encounter at the condo, and it hadn't exactly gone well. She'd been fuming at him, and that petite little woman telling him off had gotten him harder than steel. Something about knowing that she didn't want anything to do with him made him want her all that much more. He was so used to women throwing themselves at him that he didn't know what to make of her hostility—that and the fact that he'd held her against him, yet never gotten a taste of those sweet lips. Usually when a woman was that close, it ended very differently.

Imagining scenarios of him pinning her down and kissing her senseless had kept him up night after night ever since their first encounter at the condo. Even going home with a woman from Anchors hadn't fully slaked his need. She'd provided a temporary distraction from the woman he really wanted— Kenley. He was dying to peel off her clothes—not to mention peel away the layers of armor she'd put up. Not that she'd fucking give him the time of day right now, let alone a damn chance.

There wasn't much reason for her to stay in town though now that everything had died down. Lexi was readjusting after her kidnapping and had Christopher. Maybe Kenley just needed a vacation—her parents did own that condo by the beach he and Christopher had found her in. Still, it had been several weeks since the entire incident. One of these days he fully expected her to head back home. Lexi would, too, at least temporarily until her new assignment hopefully came.

"I'm not sure. Lexi's trying to talk her into moving down here, too. How crazy is that?"

"I thought she worked at the Pentagon?"

"Defense contractor in Arlington. It's a big company; I think they have plenty of contracts down here."

"Perfect," Mike muttered.

"We need to lock you two in an empty room. No, scratch that—a room with nothing but a bed. Let you fuck it out," Brent laughed.

"Jesus," Christopher groaned. "I know she wants you to stay away from her, but can't you at least try to make amends or something? Lexi and I are going to be planning a wedding soon. I don't want Lexi stressed out every time the two of you are in the same room."

"Yeah, yeah, I'm on it," Mike muttered. All he had to do was apologize to a petite, hotter-than-hell woman who loved to mouth off to him. What a freaking spectacular night this was going to turn out to be.

Chapter 2

Kenley Bristow stretched out on the lounge chair at her best friend's pool, her damp brown curls drying in the warm October sun. Lexi had all but moved in with her fiancé Christopher, and the two women were enjoying the afternoon together while the guys went to the gun range for some target practice or some other macho, I'm the manliest guy around type thing. Maybe they'd have a dick measuring contest when it was over, she thought with a smirk.

She glanced down at the black bikini she'd worn for the afternoon. It was sexy without being *too* revealing, hugging her full breasts and hanging just so on her hips. She almost wished Christopher's asshole friend Mike was around to see her in it. She would not be wearing it to the bonfire this evening, but hell if she didn't want to give him a taste of his own medicine. That guy was too damn cocky for his own good. She wanted him to see exactly what he could never have.

Kenley had raced down to Virginia Beach a month ago when Lexi had been kidnapped. While Kenley had been looking around the condo Lexi had visited, Christopher and his teammate Mike had stormed in, looking for clues. She'd come out of the bedroom and assumed one of them was Lexi's boyfriend. They both had massive builds and short, cropped hair in the standard military fashion. But the biggest guy had grabbed her as she exited the bedroom, trapping her against his solid frame, mistaking her for the enemy.

She shuddered at the memories of Mike's hard body pressing up against hers—his clean, spicy scent filling her nose, her body trembling beneath him.

She'd been angry, aroused, and frightened all at the same time. He's easily captured both of her wrists in one of his large hands, and she'd been shocked at the desire shooting through her and arousal pooling at her core. She didn't let guys manhandle her that way—she needed someone nice. Safe. Predictable.

And Mike was none of those.

Lexi's fiancé Christopher had shouted at him to release her, but Kenley had already been shaken to the core. She'd been aroused by Mike's actions. Completely turned on. His power and strength was appealing and enticing in ways she could never have imagined.

She'd always dated men who treated her with nothing but respect—who engaged in a polite kiss goodnight and maybe, after the appropriate number of dates, they'd spend the night and have safe, vanilla sex in her bed. It was nice. Unassuming. Pleasant. Maybe a bit predictable and boring. But that's what she needed—safety, stability, security. Not some guy who'd pin her against the wall in a heartbeat and have his wicked way with her.

Not that Mike had been after that exactly. He and Christopher had seen the door to her condo ajar and immediately rushed in, thinking she was somehow involved in the kidnapping. But as Mike had held her, she'd felt his thick arousal against her belly as her breasts pushed against his muscled chest. He'd wanted her, too. And that made him even more dangerous.

She'd always been attracted to guys like him from afar—rough and tumble, macho, alpha males. She worked with plenty in her job at a defense contractor in Arlington, VA. Former military guys who'd joined the private sector and active duty military officers that worked with her company on lucrative contracts with the Pentagon and Department of Defense were always around. But she never *dated* any of those guys. She stuck with what was safe, what she knew. Fellow HR employees and accounting and payroll specialists. Maybe the occasional accountant or lawyer. Safe men who had steady, boring jobs like her. Not men who could easily bench-press two of her and jumped out of airplanes for a living.

With the way her own parents had always been gone when she was growing up—traveling around the world, leaving her and her sister in the care of a nanny or some other relative, she knew she needed to find someone to make her feel safe. Secure. A Navy SEAL who deployed on dangerous missions would never be the man for her—she needed someone who'd come home every night. To give her what she never had growing up—stability. Maybe that uncertain lifestyle worked for Lexi, but it would never work for her.

"You want another drink?" Lexi asked from beside her.

"Yeah, I can grab one."

"Don't be silly. I'm getting hungry anyway. I'll bring out some chips and sodas. Sound good?"

"Sounds perfect."

"So are you definitely coming to the bonfire tonight?" Lexi asked as she stood, readjusting her blue bikini. With her jet black hair trailing down her back, she looked striking. Kenley felt positively frumpy next to her, with her head of wild, windblown curls. A dip in the pool had sounded like a great idea at the time, but now she'd look like a walking advertisement for hair products—with her being the "before" look.

"Didn't you say the whole SEAL team would be there?"

"I think so, yes."

"Then the answer's no."

"Hun, can't you move on? So Mike is kind of a jackass. The other guys are nice. And I want you to keep me company."

Kenley laughed. "You have a very hot fiancé to keep you company. Isn't that enough?" she teased.

"Yeah, but all the other guys will be there. It's not like you're crashing a date or something."

"Hey, honey," a deep, male voice rang out.

"You're back!" Lexi shouted, running across the hot pavement.

"Hi Christopher!" Kenley called out, without turning her head. There was no need to watch their welcome home, make-out session.

A shadow fell over her chair, and she glanced up. Shock coursed through her as she realized it was

Mike. She couldn't see those gorgeous blue eyes through his sunglasses, but she felt the heat of his gaze almost as if it were a caress. He scanned over her from head to toe as her breathing hitched, her chest heated, filling with something she couldn't quite explain, and warmth seeped through her. Her breathing became shallow, and she was acutely aware of the arousal pooling in her bikini bottoms. Mike hadn't even said a single word. He'd just shown up, given her a once-over, and she was melting into a puddle right in front of his eyes.

"You look hot."

"Excuse me?"

"You should cool off in the pool."

"Already done it, thanks," she said dryly, leaning back and shutting her eyes. Let him look his fill. What the hell did she care?

"I'm going in."

"It doesn't look like you have a suit on."

"Would you be opposed to skinny dipping? Of course, it's not as much fun to do it alone."

Heat surged through her at his suggestion. Certainly he wasn't proposing they go skinny dipping in broad daylight. She swallowed. Hell. The idea of Mike naked, in all his glory, was entirely too appealing. Those muscles, that thick arousal…. No. Never gonna happen.

"Yo, Christopher!" he called out.

"What's up?"

"Can I borrow a suit? Kenley and I are going swimming."

Kenley looked over to where Christopher and Lexi stood. Her eyebrows raised.

"Mike is going swimming," Kenley corrected. "I'm

quite happy here, thanks."

Mike shrugged, an easy grin spreading across his face. "Suit yourself." She looked at him, puzzled, and he winked.

Rolling her eyes, Kenley settled back into the lounge chair. A moment later, Lexi sat down beside her. "Christopher said he'll bring out some food and drinks."

"Great. Is Mike leaving?"

"Noooo. I think he went inside to change."

"What? Why?"

Lexi shrugged, putting her sunglasses back on. "He dropped Christopher off and decided to stick around. Who knows?"

"Well, he can do what he wants. I've had enough chit-chat with him for the day."

***

Mike walked back out from the apartment with a couple of bags of chips and jars of salsa. Hell. The last person he'd expected to see here was Kenley. He'd planned to drop Christopher off but had decided to come in for a quick beer. Then he'd seen her by the pool and *bam*. He couldn't bring himself to leave. She looked sexier-than-sin in that tiny little black bikini. Hell, the only thing better would be to see her in black lace. Atop his bed.

He shook his head, trying to clear his thoughts and tell his dick to stand down. A swim in the cold pool was exactly what he needed at the moment.

"Ladies," he said, setting the food on the table between then and making a beeline straight for that cold water. He dove in, surfacing a minute later. It was a little cool but nothing he wasn't used to. Hell, he was a Navy SEAL. They trained on the water all the time, in all kinds of temperatures and conditions. And the pool was a hell of a lot warmer than the Atlantic in late October.

From the far end of the pool, he saw Kenley staring at him. She couldn't see much with him standing in the deep end, but hell, just the thought of her eyes on him made him warm all over. And wasn't that a surprise. He was attracted to her, yes, but she was different than all of the other women chasing after him. She was a challenge—one he very much wanted to accept.

Christopher came down the sidewalk a moment later, two long necks in one hand and a couple of sodas in the other.

"Want a beer?" he called out to Mike.

"In a minute. Just taking a dip."

Christopher nodded and sank onto the lounge chair with Lexi.

Hell, even if Mike didn't want that sort of relationship for himself, he had to admit they looked good together. He dove back under, swimming the length of the pool. It was so short he could easily make it in one breath. He'd had years of training with the SEALs, yes, but he'd grown up on the water down in North Carolina. His family had a sweet little cottage by the beach, and he'd spent summer after summer as a kid swimming with his dad and his brothers. His mom was always content to watch from the sidelines, but it had been pretty damn picturesque. He couldn't have asked for a better childhood.

Maybe someday he'd eventually settle down, have a wife and couple of kids. He'd yet to meet the woman that lit that fire in him though, making him want something that lasted forever. Sure he'd enjoy a night or two with an attractive lady, but as for someone he wanted to commit to or spend a lifetime with? Hadn't happened yet. Didn't really suit his life as a SEAL anyway.

He surfaced, the sounds of conversation that had been distorted beneath the water ringing crystal clear.

"I can't just move down here, Lexi," Kenley said with a laugh. "My job is in Arlington."

"I know, I know. Just wishful thinking I guess. If I'm here with Christopher, how fun would it be for you to live here, too?"

Mike felt an unexpected twinge of disappointment. What did he care if or when Kenley returned to Northern Virginia? He thought she was smoking hot, but that sure as shit didn't mean he wanted to marry the woman.

Getting her into his bed would suit him just fine.

And since that seemed likely to never happen, the most he could hope for would be to steal a kiss. See if she tasted as sweet as that vanilla perfume she always had on. It drove him out of his fucking mind not knowing.

Kenley readjusted her legs on the lounge chair, and he could see the red polish on her toes. Sexy as fuck. Hell if he didn't want to toss those legs up over his shoulders, bend down, and send her straight to heaven. That wasn't exactly the type of kiss she'd allow to happen though, he thought with a smirk.

He climbed out of the pool, dripping wet, and stalked over to where she sat. Suddenly, the idea of Kenley, wet and writhing in his arms was too good to resist. If he couldn't get her into bed, at least he'd get her in the water. See how she looked dripping wet in that skimpy little bikini. She had to know men would be ogling her in that thing. Especially with the knockout body she had.

Without a word, he ducked down and scooped her up from the lounge chair as she squealed. She was so tiny compared to his large frame, he could do whatever the hell he wanted, and she wouldn't have a damn choice. Not that he'd ever take advantage of a woman, but imaging all the scenarios of him holding her curvy little body to his had him growing hard again.

"You're cold!" she cried out, squirming. "And all wet!"

He tightened his arms around her, holding her closer to his chest. Her hot body pressed up against him was enticing as hell. One little movement and that bikini top could be off, her bare breasts on display. Fuck if he didn't want to see everything Kenley had to offer.

"Put me down," she protested.

He chuckled and strode more quickly across the hot pavement.

"Mike, be nice!" Lexi called out. "Should we stop him?" she asked Christopher.

"They're fine," Christopher said, laughing. "He won't let anything happen."

Goddamn right he wouldn't let anything happen. Nor would he let her get away.

"Put me down!" Kenley said again.

Mike smirked. They had reached the deep end of the pool, and holding Kenley tightly to his wet torso, he jumped right in.

Chapter 3

Kenley panicked as the cold water surrounded them. She instinctively held her breath, but she frantically pushed against Mike, desperate for him to release her. Everything was distorted under water—her sense of sound, her sight. The pool couldn't be that deep, but it felt like they were sinking further and further away from the surface, Mike never releasing her from his iron-like grip.

Despite her parents having a condo by the beach, she'd never learned to swim. She loved splashing around in the shallow water of the ocean and walking along the shoreline, but that had been the extent of her fun on the water. Her parents were never around enough growing up to bother signing her or her sister up for swimming lessons. They'd jet off to one place or another every summer, leaving the two of them with the nanny, and she hadn't known family life to be any different. Every kid must have parents who traveled all the time and a nanny who raised them, right? They'd purchased a condo down by the beach. They'd just never been around to use it.

Her mind returned to the present as the water fully surrounded them, all sounds from the world above muffled and distant.

Mike's feet hit the bottom, and he pushed back up, kicking his legs as he propelled them back to the surface. The rise back up took even longer, and panic swelled in her chest. The sunlight became brighter as they surfaced, and she frantically flailed about, desperate for him to release her.

Mike finally let her go as she fought him, and Lexi shouted in the distance, "Kenley can't swim!"

Tears streamed down her face as Mike suddenly reappeared, his arm snaring around her waist, locking her to him. She threw her arms around his neck, her legs wrapping around his waist as he carried her toward the edge of the pool. He was so tall he could stand here, but she was barely over five feet.

"Shhh, I got you," he soothed, his mouth at her ear. She shook and clung to him, despite knowing she was safe now. Those few moments of free-falling in all that deep water had been positively terrifying. She couldn't swim, so she'd never once jumped into a deep pool of water like that. She never would again, either.

Her back met the rough edge of the pool, and still Mike held her to him. His muscular arms were locked around her, and she foolishly cried into his neck.

"I'm sorry, Kenley," he apologized. "Are you okay?"

Finally she lifted her head. Concerned blue eyes met her gaze, and Mike swiped a tear running down her cheek. Despite her fear moments ago, it felt good to be in his arms. Too good. He was walls of solid muscle, bigger and stronger than most other men. He held her so closely to him, she knew nothing bad would happen whenever he was around. Even though he was the one who'd jumped into the pool with her, he'd helped her. Carried her back to the side. Held her as she cried.

"You can't swim?"

"No," she whispered.

"I'm sorry; I never would've done that—"

She nodded, another tear slipping down her face.

"Please don't cry," he said, his voice catching.

He wiped her tears away, and they stared at each other a moment as their heat intermingled. Suddenly the cool water lapping around them felt very, very hot. Or maybe it was the solid male that was holding her. Mike shifted slightly, his arousal hitting her exactly where she wanted him. He was just as turned on at their wet bodies pressed together as she was. Being in Mike's arms was suddenly the absolute only place she wanted to be.

Mike leaned in and kissed her, and she momentarily forgot how to breathe.

He was gentle and sweet, and he kept up his tender kisses as she tightened her hold. Her breasts pushed against his broad chest, and her hardened nipples rubbed against him through her thin bikini top. Pushing her back ever-so-slightly into the wall, he ground his erection into her core.

She gasped as he rubbed against her, exactly where she needed him. He felt so damn good, she didn't know what to make of it. She barely knew him. She didn't make out with guys she'd just met. They'd never so much as had dinner together or gone out on a date, and he was grinding against her in the pool like she was his.

Mike's hands slid to her bottom, palming it as he pulled her tighter against him. The tips of his fingers slid just beneath the fabric, and she gasped at his hands on her bare flesh. It felt so good having Mike touch her, kiss her, control all of their movements. Their bodies fit perfectly together. His muscles and hard planes up against all her soft curves felt like pure magic.

Christopher cleared his throat in the distance, and Kenley abruptly jerked back in Mike's arms. Although they were mostly covered in water, their make-out session had obviously not gone unnoticed. Of course not. She'd flailed about like an idiot and then cried as Mike came to her rescue. Well, he'd also been the cause of her torment in the first place.

Kenley untangled herself from Mike as he loosened his grip but still held her securely in his arms. She wasn't sure if he didn't want to let her go because it meant ending their heated make-out session or because he was still concerned about her near drowning. Well, she probably hadn't been that close to drowning with Mike, Christopher, and Lexi at the pool, but it sure the hell felt that way.

"Kenley—"

"I have to go." She bolted for the ladder, climbing out of the pool. Mike's heated gaze slid over her entire body, and she shuddered. He remained where she'd left him, no doubt in an effort to conceal that massive hard-on he was sporting.

"I've got to go, guys," she said, grabbing her towel from where Christopher and Lexi sat with amused expressions on their faces. Scratch that—Christopher looked amused, Lexi looked in disbelief.

"I better see you at the bonfire tonight," Lexi said. She leaned in closer. "Because I need details!"

Kenley flushed, ignoring Christopher and grabbing Lexi firmly by the arm as she dragged her away. "Not a word about this. Ever. It was a one-time thing."

"Right," Lexi laughed. "I'll see you tonight."

***

Kenley tugged her curly brown hair back into a loose ponytail as she stepped onto the soft sand later that evening. Anxiety churned through her, but she shook it off, telling herself she was being silly. Why should she be worried about running into Mike? They'd go back to the way things were—with her ignoring him—and she could spend the night drinking and talking with her best friend. Problem solved.

She shuddered as she recalled Mike's heated kisses in the pool today. The way those full lips moved over hers were like they were made to kiss a woman. Everywhere. If Mike's arousal had been any indication, he'd be happy to acquiesce. Hell, if Lexi and Christopher hadn't been there, who knows what would've happened. She didn't even know what had gotten into her. Something about him stoked this untamable urge inside her to let him kiss and devour her. To do whatever the hell he wanted, because it felt so damn right.

She slipped off her sandals, allowing them to dangle in one hand, as she walked around shells and padded toward the bonfire in the distance. She took a deep breath, steeling herself. Lexi would have questions. Christopher would have questions. Mike would probably show up and seek her out. She'd just have to change the subject and move on. The quicker she did, the quicker they would. And then everyone could forget about the entire embarrassing incident at the pool today.

The sea air assaulted her senses, filled with salt and brine, and the breeze blowing in off the ocean made her wish she'd worn more than shorts and a thin tank top. At least she had a cozy sweater tied around her waist for later. And it would be warmer by the fire, she reasoned. Maybe she could find a hunky, single SEAL to snuggle up to—*right*. She certainly wasn't getting up close and personal with Mike again. Ever. And that meant the rest of the guys were off limits, too. Not that she'd ever really noticed anyone but him. It was unnerving, really, how he got to her that way.

Kenley kicked the soft sand as she walked, watching it fall back down. She'd come to the beach every weekend over the past month. She liked it here, even if her stay was just temporary. But nothing she needed for the future she'd mapped out could be found here on this beach—no matter how frustratingly tempting some of the men may seem.

She could just make out Lexi and Christopher, along with another couple, as they set up chairs and blankets around the bonfire. *Damn it.* She'd left her cozy flannel blanket in the car. She didn't feel like trekking back across the beach and down the block to retrieve it. Maybe Lexi had an extra one she could use.

A cooler sat beside the fire, and as she got closer,

she could see a woman pulling out hotdogs and skewers for them to roast over the roaring flames. A massive man walked up from the other direction, hauling another cooler. He set it down and began pulling beers out and passing them to the other guys.

"Hey, darlin'," he said as she approached.

She smiled back, trying to remember the guy's name. There were six men on the SEAL team, and to make matters even more complicated, each of them had a nickname as well. They usually addressed each other by their given name in crowds like this, but it was no wonder she couldn't keep half of them straight. Aside from Christopher and Mike, the other guys kind of blurred together.

"Kenley!" Lexi called out, rushing over to give her a hug. Her dark hair swung as she swooped in, and the smile on her face could've lit up the entire beach. "I thought for sure you wouldn't show!"

"I almost didn't."

"Oh come on, no one cares about you and Mike."

Kenley pointedly raised her eyebrows.

"What?"

"It took you exactly two point five seconds to mention him."

Lexi shrugged. "Okay, so maybe I care. And want details of what exactly went down. But these other guys? Trust me when I say they couldn't care less."

"I guess," Kenley said. Although she felt like all eyes were on her, absolutely no one was looking at her. Not even Christopher, who seemed more concerned with stoking the fire. Maybe tonight would be okay after all.

"Anyway, I'm glad you decided to come. We'll do stuff with the guys tonight and then have our girls only day tomorrow."

"I heard that," Christopher joked as he walked over.

Kenley smiled at her friend's handsome fiancé. Why couldn't the other guys all be sweet like Christopher? "I'm sure you can spare her for a little while, right?" she asked him with a wink.

"Maybe," he said, giving Lexi a chaste kiss on the cheek.

Kenley raised her eyebrows.

"Let me introduce you to everyone else," Lexi said. "I know you met some of them before—"

"Trust me, I can't keep half of the guys straight."

"That's Matthew, Patrick, and Rebecca," Lexi said, pointing out the others. "And you already know Christopher," she joked, snuggling against him as a breeze blew off the water.

Christopher's gaze quickly scanned over Kenley as he wrapped an arm around Lexi's shoulders. "You might be cold in that."

Kenley had noticed when she walked up that everyone else had on jeans or long pants, plus long-sleeved shirts and jackets or sweatshirts. It was a little late to do anything about her outfit choice now though. "I figured we're at the beach," she said with a shrug.

"We always come down here in the summer," Lexi explained. "She'll be fine—we have a bonfire. So how's work going anyway?" she asked, turning her attention back to Kenley. "Will you be in town much longer?"

"I think we've nailed down the specifics for the new contract in Norfolk," Kenley said, referring to the town neighboring Virginia Beach. Norfolk housed the largest naval base in the world, and there were always multiple defense contractors bidding on lucrative contracts with the Navy. Her own company included. "I've been interviewing candidates all week to fill the extra positions. Another week or so and I'll probably be heading back up to Arlington."

"Awww, that soon? I'll miss you!"

Kenley laughed as her gaze swept to Christopher. "Isn't this guy enough company?"

"Damn straight," Christopher joked, pulling his fiancée closer. She looked more than happy to melt into his embrace, and Kenley sighed. When was the last time a man had made her feel that way?

"Just so you know, Mike's coming tonight," Christopher suddenly said.

"Perfect," Kenley groaned, rolling her eyes. She knew the entire team had been invited, but a part of her had been secretly hoping that Mike would be a no-show. Especially after this afternoon. She'd bolted from the pool without so much as a goodbye, and knowing him, he wouldn't leave it at that. Besides, he was way too attractive and unnerving for his own good. She didn't like the way her brain always short-circuited around him, making her feel like a school girl with a crush on the captain of the football team. Why couldn't he just fade into the background when he was around like all the other men on the SEAL team? Instead, it was like he was a magnet, drawing her to him, and no matter how hard she tried to pull away, resistance was futile.

Lexi laughed. "Sweetie, come on. It sure seemed like you guys kissed and made up earlier. Can't you move on? Maybe play nice for the night?"

"Hey, you guys made it!" Patrick called out from

29

where he stood helping Rebecca pull food from the cooler. He was tall and massive as well, with a snug fitting shirt that hugged all his muscles and cool, ice blue eyes.

"I hope you're hungry," Rebecca said. "We brought enough food to feed an army."

"Or a hungry SEAL team," Patrick joked.

Kenley glanced over her shoulder to see Mike approaching along with another guy. Her heart skittered to a stop as a chill raced down her spine, immediately followed by a flush that washed over her skin. Her entire body was pulsing with awareness, every nerve ending tingling. She was frozen in place, unable to move or even look away as the guys approached. Blue eyes nailed her with a gaze. Just perfect. Now she'd been caught gawking.

"Are you okay?" Lexi whispered.

Kenley glanced back at her friend. "I'm fine," she huffed. "Just because he's here doesn't mean I need to talk to him. Or associate with him." She hastened a glance back.

"Or look at him," Christopher teased.

Kenley could feel her face flaming. "I was just trying to figure out who he was with," she said lightly. "You can't expect me to remember who everyone is."

Christopher raised his eyebrows as Lexi playfully elbowed him in the side.

"That's just Brent," Christopher said. "Don't worry about him."

Kenley resisted the urge to shudder. If anyone freaked her out more than Mike, it was him. The vibe he gave off was unpleasant at best and predatory at worst. He was like a lion stalking a lamb and made Mike seem pretty damn tame in comparison. From the stories Lexi had told her about Brent, he was with a different woman every night of the week. While she was up for some excitement in her life, he was way too far at the opposite end of the spectrum for her liking.

Brent mumbled a hello to them but sauntered over to the cooler to grab a beer from Matthew. They waved at another group of people in the distance— one guy with a group of women. Kenley watched them, puzzled.

"Evan's girlfriend, Alison, is bringing some of her nurse friends tonight," Mike explained as he stopped at her side, his voice deep. She turned back to meet his searching blue gaze. He hadn't even bothered to say hello to her. The fact that Lexi discreetly dragged Christopher away at that exact moment didn't escape her notice. She'd have to kill her friend later for leaving her alone with Mike.

"Looking to meet someone?" Kenley couldn't help but retort. She felt her face burning. What the hell was wrong with her? Who cared if he met some chick and made out with her all night by the roaring fire? It sure the hell wasn't her concern.

"Not exactly," Mike said, his voice gruff. His six feet plus towered above her own petite frame, and as she took in his cropped dark hair and chiseled features, she had to admit to herself that he was handsome. Not that she'd ever tell him that.

His bulk was contained beneath a long-sleeved tee shirt that stretched across his massive chest and broad shoulders. His pecs stood out against the snug fabric, and she knew exactly what the washboard abs concealed beneath his clothes looked like. Well-worn jeans clung to his muscular thighs, and work boots encased his feet. The man looked mouth-watering from head to toe. Not that she'd be sampling a taste.

"Boots?" she asked.

Mike shrugged. "It's mid-October, not July. Are you warm enough?" he asked, suddenly seeming concerned.

"I'm fine," she said, wishing she'd thought to wear jeans at least. Bare feet, shorts, and a tank top didn't seem quite appropriate for a fall beach bonfire. Oh well. Too late now. She'd just leave if she got too cold as the night wore on. She unwrapped her sweater from around her waist and tugged it over her head, suddenly feeling naked beneath Mike's penetrating gaze. The heat that filled her chest was from the warmth of her sweater—not her reaction to Mike. Not at all.

Mike was watching her closely when she re-emerged. "Can we talk for a minute?" he asked, looking uncomfortable. He shifted from side to side.

"Kenley, over here!" Lexi called, waving a skewered hot dog in the air. Christopher grabbed her from behind at that exact moment, and she shrieked happily.

Kenley glanced back at Mike, feeling like the few feet between them was the expanse of the entire ocean. Aside from the pool this afternoon, she'd seen him exactly once since their encounter at the condo, and it had been just as awkward as tonight. The fact that her heart was skittering to a stop in her chest as she gazed up at him wasn't helping matters. Why was her body responding to this man whose aggression and assertiveness was so completely wrong for her? Maybe she was interested in dating someone different, but he was too many steps in the wrong direction. Way too far off the course she'd planned for her life. "Uh, maybe later. See ya."

She turned and hurriedly walked away, Mike's spicy scent still lingering in the air. That man smelled positively scrumptious. How was she supposed to relax and enjoy the evening knowing he was here—and worse, knowing he thought they needed some heart-to-heart? She wasn't even sure what he wanted. Was he going to apologize? Call a truce? Haul her off into the dunes and kiss her senseless?

She flushed as she imagined Mikes lips on her skin, the scruff of his five o'clock shadow rubbing against her sensitive flesh. His thick arousal rubbing against her sex was still fresh in her mind, and a part of her wanted to continue exactly where they'd left off. To see just how good Mike could make her feel. Not that that was ever, *ever* going to happen. This afternoon was a one-time deal, and the sooner she communicated that to Mike, the better.

So naturally, she was walking away from him and toward her best friend. Because that would resolve everything.

Lexi was getting some food for her, so Kenley grabbed a beer from the open cooler and sank into the sand beside her. The wall of heat that washed over her from the bonfire felt good. She stretched her legs out in the sand, enjoying the warmth on her bare skin. Lexi handed her a plate, and she could feel Mike's burning gaze from behind. No time like the present to start ignoring him. It might be easier to ignore the sun in the sky than the way his presence lit up her world, but she was willing to try.

"What was that about?" Lexi asked, nodding in Mike's direction.

Kenley blew out a sigh. "Who knows. He said he wanted to talk."

"About the condo or the pool?"

"Don't know. Don't care."

"He is sorry, you know. About the condo, I mean. Christopher said he was really worried he'd scared you."

Kenley let out a bitter laugh. "He sure had a damn funny way of showing it. Your fiancé had to order him to release me—and I was in my own home!"

"I know. Those guys are used to neutralizing the threat, controlling the situation. He reacted without thinking. They were just worried about me, you know?"

Kenley wrapped an arm around her best friend's shoulder. "I know. So was I. That didn't mean I appreciated him scaring me like that."

"Ladies," Christopher said, approaching them with two cooked hotdogs, still sizzling on the skewers.

"Such a gentleman," Kenley teased.

"Thanks hun," Lexi said, leaning forward to give him a kiss.

Those two were so sweet it practically hurt to look at them. Kenley hastened a glance back in Mike's direction and found him still watching her intently. He nodded once and then turned his attention back to his friends. What was his deal anyway? He didn't need to keep tabs on her. They weren't friends. They weren't anything.

She grabbed a fork and slid the hotdog from the skewer and onto a bun, taking a bite. It was just the right amount of charred and tasted completely delicious, or maybe she was just starving. Come to think of it, she never did have her snack or soda at the pool earlier. She reached over and helped herself to a few of the side dishes spread out by the cooler, filling her plate. Everything tasted better down by the water. The sea air, salt, and sand just made life better in general. It was going to be tough returning to DC in another week or so when she'd finished hiring for their new contract. But her job, apartment, and life were there. She had no reason to stick around here longer than necessary.

"Are either of you ready for another hotdog?" Christopher asked as he polished off his second.

"Not me, thanks," Kenley said. "I haven't even finished my first one yet."

"No thanks, hun," Lexi said.

"No biggie, more for us men," Christopher said with a wink.

Evan sauntered over, grabbing plates for him and Alison. Christopher loaded him up, and Kenley noticed Evan's plate was also piled high with food. With the grueling workouts and deployments they went on, it was no wonder they needed to eat so much to keep up their strength. She had a feeling they could each polish off more food in one sitting than she could eat in a week. Not that she was complaining in the least about their muscular physiques. Lexi and the other women were lucky indeed.

"Thanks, man," Evan said, walking back over to where he'd left Alison and her friends. Kenley couldn't help but notice that all the single men on the SEAL team were congregated around the pretty nurses. Big surprise. Brent had a huge grin on his face, and Matthew had casually slung his arm around the shoulders of one of the women. Mike wasn't with anyone in particular, but he sure didn't look too uncomfortable amidst all the female company.

"You should go talk to him," Lexi prodded.

"Who?"

Lexi rolled her eyes. "You've been looking Mike's way every couple of minutes."

"He's got plenty of women over there to keep him company. I don't need to get in the middle of that."

"I'm pretty sure you wouldn't be in the middle. Didn't you say he wanted to talk?"

Kenley blew out a sigh. "It doesn't matter. I'll be leaving in a week or so, and then I won't have to worry about him again."

"He'll be at the wedding you know."

"Have you set a date?" Kenley asked.

"No, not yet," Lexi sighed. "There's too much going on. Hopefully sometime next summer."

"Well then I don't have anything to worry about. I'll be totally over him by then."

"Over him?" Lexi asked, raising her eyebrows.

"Over being mad at him," Kenley hastened to explain.

Lexi shook her head in disbelief and pulled Christopher's jacket around her shoulders. "This is a great night," she said wistfully as the bonfire crackled in front of them.

"It is. Thanks again for inviting me."

"Hey, you're practically family. So if I'm part of Christopher's SEAL team family now, then you are, too."

Kenley nodded and absentmindedly took a swig of her beer, her gut churning. Good friends. A beach bonfire. Food. Alcohol. So why was she suddenly feeling so melancholy?

Chapter 4

Mike cursed under his breath as Kenley caught him watching her. She looked so small and fragile in those little shorts, sandals carelessly tossed on the sand beside her. The sweater she'd pulled on wouldn't provide much shield against the wind—not with that skimpy little tank top she was wearing beneath. He groaned at the way she'd looked in it—all womanly curves, with the swells of her breasts peeking above the top. And hell—he knew exactly how soft she was. How good those lush breasts felt pressing against his chest. Her small body against his hard frame had felt damn near like heaven.

And hell if she didn't look like perfection right now. Those toned legs were stretched out in front of her as she basked in the firelight—they looked so silky smooth, he'd kill to pull her off alone for a few minutes. They'd sneak off behind some of the dunes, he'd haul her onto his lap, grinding his hard-on against her, and he'd run his hands roughly up and down those gorgeous legs as he kissed her senseless. Those shorts were so short he could tease and caress the tender flesh on her inner thighs, giving her a taste of what a night with him promised to be like. Of just how good he could make her feel.

Not that any of that scenario was entirely appropriate given the circumstances. Or likely to ever happen.

The firelight danced across Kenley's skin, and a few wisps of that curly hair had escaped her ponytail and framed her face. He was dying to give just one of those curls a gentle tug to see how she responded. Then he'd tuck it gently back behind her ear, whispering all the ways he wanted to get to know her better. Her sweet lips looked rosier than ever in the warm light, and damn if he wasn't dying for just one more taste.

She shifted as she finished her food, wrapping her sweater-clad arms around her shapely legs. His groin tightened as he watched her.

The possessive, protective alpha male in him wanted to go to her. To take care of her. The need to watch out for others was engrained in his DNA, just like it was in all the guys on his SEAL team. Sure, he wouldn't exactly be fighting off any terrorists or drug lords tonight on the beach, but making sure Kenley was safe and secure felt like a damn good idea. She must be freezing out here, and the air was only going to get colder as the night wore on. Hell if he didn't wish he had some right to worry about her. Some claim to her that made it his duty to protect and care for Kenley.

That was probably the last thing on Earth she

wanted with the way they'd met a few weeks ago. With the way she'd run off at the pool earlier. He didn't regret his actions, but hell. Was it too much for a guy to want a damn chance?

Grumbling, he wandered over and grabbed a beer from the cooler.

"I've got dibs on the blonde," Brent said, eyes flaring as he eyed the nurse friends Alison had brought along. She was currently introducing them to the couples seated around the bonfire, but one of them kept sneaking peeks in their direction.

"I'm not looking to meet anyone tonight," Mike muttered.

"I take it your conversation with Kenley didn't go too well?" Brent smirked.

"Never happened." He took a long pull from his beer. Damn that tasted good. He could go for some food, too, but now that Kenley was seated beside the fire, he didn't feel like walking over to where she was. Hell. What was he—in eighth grade or something? Avoiding the pretty girls? If they were going to be around each other he needed to smooth the waters—for her sake and his.

"And, another one bites the dust," Matthew drawled, following Mike's gaze over to the bonfire.

Mike ignored him, finally tearing his eyes away from Kenley, and said hello to Evan and Alison as they walked up with her friends. Brent tugged the blonde off to get her a drink. She giggled as he complimented her, and Mike rolled his eyes. That guy always had the women eating out of his hand.

A cute little brunette sidled up to him, and he tried to engage in some polite conversation without completely brushing her off. She was a nurse. She loved military men. Got it. From the corner of his eye, he watched Kenley rise and walk over to one of the coolers to grab a drink. She shivered as she stepped away from the fire, and he bit back a curse. "Excuse me," he said to the attractive woman in front of him. "I need to go grab something from my car."

"Need some company?" she asked, a flirty smile on her pink lips.

"Nah, I'll be back in ten."

He didn't miss the hurt expression on her face, but he didn't care. No sense in leading her on when the chances of him taking a woman home tonight were zilch. Not unless Kenley had a sudden change of heart, which was doubtful. Breaking down her walls would be like melting an iceberg—not exactly a task to be accomplished in one evening.

Mike offered a brief explanation to Evan and Matthew about grabbing something from his vehicle and then jogged off down the beach. He kept a sweatshirt and some PT gear in the back of his SUV. It was going to drive him crazy watching Kenley shivering all night long. And if he couldn't be the one to warm her up with his body heat, then at least his sweatshirt could. Masculine pride swelled in his chest at the idea of Kenley in his clothes. Hell, he'd prefer to see her in nothing at all. That petite little thing was a knockout—he'd felt her curves against him and was dying to see the whole package. Preferably sprawled out on his bed.

He made it to his vehicle in under five minutes and grabbed a clean sweatshirt from the back. It would be huge on her, but she'd be warm. Hell, she'd look cute wearing his oversized clothes. Even if it did hide her curves, that fact that she'd be wearing something of his made him feel about ten feet tall. He didn't think any of the other single guys on his team had their eye on Kenley, but if this helped stake his claim and kept the other guys away, he wouldn't complain.

Shutting the trunk, Mike set the alarm and then jogged back to the quiet north end of the beach where they'd set up for the evening. He could see the silhouettes of his buddies and the women in the light of the fire. It was dark down by the water, away from the lights dotting the boardwalk and coming from the restaurants and hotels. As he got closer, he came to a stop and looked around, puzzled. Lexi was snuggled next to Christopher, right where he'd last seen them. Rebecca and Patrick had a blanket wrapped around their shoulders as they ate by the fire. Brent and the blonde were off to the side drinking beers—as were Evan, Alison, Matthew, and the other woman.

He scanned the group again, making sure he hadn't somehow missed her.

Kenley was gone.

***

Kenley shivered as she hurried back down the beach. The sand was cold beneath her feet, and she wished she had on socks and sneakers. Not to mention long pants. The wind blowing in off the water cut right through the loose knit of her sweater, and goose bumps spread over her flesh. Apparently she should've paid closer attention to the October weather before dressing for the evening. The summer nights she'd spent on the beach were sweltering—this felt more like autumn back home. She'd be chilled to the bone by the time she got to her car.

Blowing out a sigh, she hurried along the sand. Lexi had been disappointed that she'd left early, but she wouldn't exactly be lonely with Christopher keeping her warm. With the two of them hanging out around the fire with Patrick and Rebecca, Kenley had felt like the fifth wheel anyway. She didn't exactly need to be there beside the happy couples. Or to stand around with Alison's friends chatting up the single men on the SEAL team.

Glancing back, she could make out the bonfire in the distance. She could always drive home, grab something warmer, then come back, but that almost seemed like it was more hassle than it was worth. She'd just—

"Ow!"

Kenley muttered under her breath as she accidentally stepped on a seashell, cursing as it cut into her foot. She stopped for a moment, glancing down. It hurt but hadn't broken her skin. At least she was almost back to the boardwalk. She readjusted her array of curls, tucking in the strands that had broken free of the ponytail. She probably looked like a crazed woman hurrying down the beach like this—hair wildly blowing about, muttering to herself as she stepped on inanimate objects. Freaking perfect.

She gingerly stepped onto the boardwalk, brushing the sand from her bare feet. It was going to hurt like hell walking back to her car like this. Maybe she'd just sit down for a few minutes until she felt better. She balanced on one leg, tugging on a sandal. A man jogging by with his dog nodded at her, and she politely said hello before pulling her other sandal on.

See, that guy didn't even *know* her but had said hi. Apparently that was too much for what's-his-name, who just started talking to her like they were buddies or something. Honestly, what was his problem? Mike had barely spoken to her this evening before abruptly leaving. So much for the big talk he needed to have with her. The minute she'd finished eating and stood up to grab another beer from the cooler, he'd literally turned and run off down the beach. Not that she'd expected them to become best buds or something, but damn. Turning and running the other way didn't bode well.

Kenley blew out a sigh. She couldn't be friends with anyone that hot anyway. She'd be drooling over him while he had some new gorgeous woman on his arm. Not that she cared if he dated anyone. He could date every damn woman in Virginia Beach if he wanted. Their kiss earlier today had been nothing but a big, fat mistake. So there was that, too.

At least he didn't take one of those women with him when he left. Alison seemed nice enough, so she assumed her friends were. But the thought that she'd brought them along to meet the single guys on Mike's SEAL team—Mike included—didn't sit well with her. And wasn't that a surprise. She was sure wasting a lot of time thinking about a man she couldn't stand. Hmmph.

She gingerly walked over to the bench and sank down, wondering if her foot would stop bothering her in a few more minutes. In the meantime she'd just have to sit here and freeze a little longer. She shivered again and wrapped her arms around herself, trying to stay warm.

"Kenley!"

She started and looked up to see Mike himself walking her direction. Had he chased after her down the beach? It was amazing that he'd restrained himself and not tackled her in the sand or something. Wasn't that his MO? Shoot first, ask questions later?

Crap. What if something was wrong with Lexi? Here she was thinking about what an ass he was, and he'd come running after her. But wait—hadn't he left already?

Mike stepped onto the boardwalk and was at the bench in two long strides, looking tall and dangerous as he towered above her. He gripped a sweatshirt tightly in his hand, and his gaze slid to where she absentmindedly rubbed her injured foot.

"Are you okay?" he asked, voice gruff.

"Fine," she said, getting to her feet. She winced as she put pressure on the injured one.

Mike stepped closer, and she waved him off. "I just stepped on a shell in the dark. I'm fine."

"Why'd you leave?"

"I was cold. Why'd you leave?" she asked, putting her hands on her hips as she glared up at him. Seriously, what was his problem? He chased her all the way here to ask why she'd left?

"I went to get you a sweatshirt."

"You—wait, what?"

"I had an extra one in my car, and you looked cold."

Right on cue, she shivered in the night air. "Here, take it," he commanded. Warily, she met his gaze. His jaw clenched as he watched her, his chiseled, masculine features almost too much to bear. How could someone who was so handsome also act like such a jerk half the time? It just wasn't fair. She hesitated, unsure of what to do. Why did it feel like taking his sweatshirt meant more than borrowing a damn piece of clothing?

His blue eyes softened as he watched her. "Go on, you're cold," he said, his voice deep. Maybe it was some sort of peace offering. What did she care? Reluctantly, she reached out to take the proffered sweatshirt. She was freezing. And even if Mike was kind of a jerk, it was still sort of sweet that he'd run back to grab it from his car and then chased after her. All the way back to the boardwalk.

She slipped into the oversized, soft cotton, and holy hell. It even smelled like him. Like man and spice and everything oh so nice. She resisted the urge to inhale deeply and wrap her arms around herself. That would feel too much like being in Mike's arms. Not that she wanted that to happen again.

He jerked his head back toward the beach. "Are you coming back?"

"Yeah, I guess. Lexi was bummed that I left early."

Mike nailed her with a gaze. "She wasn't the only one."

Kenley's heart beat faster in her chest, and she raised her eyebrows, trying to play it cool.

"I wanted to talk to you, remember? I didn't think I'd have to run after you down the beach to do so."

"Sorry, I just…." Why was she apologizing to him? She didn't owe him an explanation. She didn't owe him anything.

"I'm the one who's sorry. I know we didn't get off to the best start when I frightened you at your condo, and I never would've done that if we hadn't been searching for Lexi and her kidnappers. My SEAL team is trained to be alert and subdue any threats. Christopher and I were both on edge with Lexi missing, and you'd left the door open. I wouldn't just barge into a woman's place and grab her like that otherwise. I know you were terrified."

Kenley swallowed and nodded. "I get it, all right? I was worried about Lexi, too—that's why I raced down here from Arlington."

Mike nodded and cleared his throat. "And this afternoon—I swear I had no idea you couldn't swim. You've got that condo by the beach, and you and Lexi were spending the afternoon at the pool, I just assumed—"

"Forget it, okay?"

"If you're sure you're all right. I would never do anything to hurt you—or any woman for that matter."

Kenley shrugged. "You didn't know. It's fine."

Mike nailed her with a gaze. "And afterward, with that kiss…."

"I said I just wanted to forget about the whole thing. Can you just drop it?"

Mike's features hardened. He looked like he wanted to say something else but didn't. "Let's head back. I still haven't eaten, and I think Patrick and Rebecca were getting ready to roast marshmallows." He held out his arm, and Kenley looked at it hesitantly.

"Come on. I don't want you tripping on any more shells. I brought a flashlight, too."

He turned it on as if to prove his point and waited for her. Against her better judgment, Kenley finally slipped her arm through Mike's, trying not to gasp at the solid strength of him. Even beneath their layers of clothing, she could feel his rock solid strength. Memories of his body pressed against hers washed over her, and she shook her head, feeling dazed. She couldn't have recounted half of what she'd done this week, but she remembered every second Mike had pinned her against him. His scent. His strength. His ragged breaths. His arousal. She swallowed, trying to think of anything else.

They stepped off the boardwalk and into the sand, Kenley moving stiffly beside him. Mike's presence at her side both reassured and unnerved her. He'd never harm her, but thoughts of all the ways his powerful body could move over her left her feeling uneasy. What the hell was wrong with her? She didn't want to sleep with him. She didn't even want to walk back to the bonfire with him. But Lexi had invited her tonight. Now that she had something to keep her warm, what excuse did she have for bailing out early?

"You warmer now?"

"Uh, yeah. Thanks."

Mike made a low sound in the back of his throat, which she assumed was some sort of grunt of affirmation. Glancing up, she met his gaze and was shocked to see arousal in his eyes. Hastily, she pulled her arm from his. Mike's jaw stiffened.

The man she'd seen jogging earlier on the boardwalk with his dog was coming back on the sand, barely visible in the beam of Mike's flashlight. His dog barked and suddenly broke free, running right toward her. Kenley shrieked, and Mike pushed her behind him, shouting a command to the dog. She cowered behind him, pressing against his back, as Mike's hand gripped her waist. Her forehead rested against his shoulder blades, and her hands splayed flat across Mike's lower back. She probably looked like an idiot hiding behind Mike, but at the moment she was too terrified to care.

The jogger ran toward them with the broken leash, apologizing. Mike released her and held onto the dog's collar as the owner roughly tied the leash back together, providing an impromptu solution. He apologized again and continued on his way as Mike turned back toward Kenley.

She trembled as she watched him, embarrassment coursing through her.

"You don't like dogs?"

"Not when they're jumping on me. Or running at me in full-on attack mode." Her voice shook, and she looked away from Mike's gaze.

"Hey, it's okay," he said, stepping closer. "I'd never let anything happen to you."

Kenley looked back at him, puzzled. "You barely even know me."

Mike shrugged. "I'm a Navy SEAL. It's what we do. Usually we're operating on foreign terrain, not rescuing women from swimming pools or friendly dogs on the beach, but hey."

"Stop making fun of me."

"I'm not," he said, suddenly serious. "I want you to know you're safe with me."

"Just forget it," she muttered, brushing past him. How humiliating. First he'd had to come to her rescue in a swimming pool of all places, now he'd seen she was frightened of barking dogs running her way. Jesus. She really should just call it a night. And make it a point of staying away from wherever he was in the future.

Mike caught her elbow lightly, and she glanced back at him. "How many times do I need to apologize?"

"You don't; everything's fine."

He released her but stepped so close that she had to tilt her head back to meet his gaze. No parts of their bodies were touching, but the electricity sizzling between them was enough to set every nerve ending in her body on fire. He was tall. Broad. Strong. His very presence was making her dizzy. The flashlight beamed down at their feet, and she could barely see his expression in the moonlight. The waves crashed against the shore, pounding in rhythm with the blood rushing through her veins. She could hear the laughter of their friends in the distance, see the dim lights of the boardwalk they'd left behind, but at this moment, her entire existence felt like it hinged on him.

Two military jets flew in from the ocean, the sound of them announcing their imminent appearance. They soared over the sand where they stood, flying high above the city of Virginia Beach. Their engines roared across the night sky, and Kenley wondered what they saw from above. She and Mike were so small and insignificant standing here on the beach—barely anything at all.

"They're from Naval Air Station Oceana," Mike commented as she watched them. They looked so tiny high up in the air, their lights allowing her to follow their path. It was a clear night, and she watched as they screamed across the sky and eventually disappeared from sight.

Mike moved a fraction of an inch closer to her, and she stepped back. He reached out and tucked a stray strand of hair behind her ear, the heat from his touch and sparks flying between them almost unbearable. "Why are you afraid of me?"

"I'm not scared of you," she retorted.

"No?"

"No," she said stubbornly.

His hands came to her waist, and she leapt back from him like she'd been burned. Her heart pounded furiously in her chest, and she turned and hurried toward the bonfire, Mike wordlessly catching up to her in an instant. What was he trying to do? For a moment there, she'd thought he was going to kiss her again. As if this afternoon at the pool had actually meant something. As if anything else would ever happen between them.

She clenched her jaw, willing herself not to cry. There was heat between them, yes, but Mike was a thousand different ways wrong for her. Maybe they'd have fun, but then he'd move on with the next girl or leave on his next mission, and she'd be left where she always had been. On her own.

The remainder of the walk back was silent. A loaded silence. Mike's hand brushed against hers once, and she quickly jerked away. He didn't try to touch or comfort her again after that.

Lexi's jaw dropped when she saw Kenley in Mike's oversized sweatshirt, but Kenley waved her off. Seriously. Couldn't a guy do a nice thing without the whole world assuming they were together or something? They would never be anything to each other. She took the roasted marshmallow and s'mores fixings that Rebecca offered her, tears smarting in her eyes as she rejoined Lexi and the others.

"Are you okay?" Lexi asked, looking concerned.

"Never better," Kenley said, taking a bite of the chocolate marshmallow gooeyness. Man, she could eat about ten of these with the sucky night she was having. She brushed some stray graham cracker crumbs from her lap, taking a second bite as Lexi watching her intently.

Kenley swallowed as Mike appeared and grabbed a plate and some food, sending her a loaded glance. She turned to Lexi and whispered, "Let's talk tomorrow, okay?"

"Okay, hun," Lexi said, wrapping an arm around Kenley's shoulders and giving her a quick hug. "I'm glad you decided to come back though."

Mike wandered back over to Matthew, Brent, and the nurses to eat his dinner, leaving Kenley sitting alone by the fire with the other couples. They laughed and enjoyed talking, drinking, and eating around the flames, but Kenley spent the rest of the night ignoring the brooding Navy SEAL whose eyes never left her.

Chapter 5

"So what was that about last night?" Christopher asked the next afternoon. Mike gripped his end of the sofa more tightly, his biceps flexing, as they carried the heavy piece of furniture the last few steps across the living room of Christopher's apartment.

They set it back on the carpeted floor and Mike straightened, brushing his hands off as he eyed the sofa's new spot under the windows. With Lexi moving in with Christopher soon, somehow he'd gotten roped into helping rearrange the damn apartment. Not exactly his ideal way to spend a Sunday afternoon, but at least football would be on soon. "What was what about? This thing's off-center," he said, cocking his head.

Christopher shoved the sofa two more inches. "The whole song and dance with Kenley. You chased her down the beach, she returned wearing your sweatshirt, but then you two didn't speak the rest of the night."

"The hell if I know," Mike muttered, turning away and scanning the messy room. Boxes were stacked in the corner, the furniture was in disarray, and Christopher looked happier than ever. Good. He deserved it. But as for Mike's own problems with Kenley? What the hell did he know? He'd tried to apologize to Kenley, even tried to do something nice for her, but the woman was still mad. Not to mention completely freaked out around him. There wasn't much to tell. She'd stayed glued to Lexi's side the entire night, wearing his sweatshirt, as everyone had apparently noticed. But had she glanced his way? Tried to talk to him? Not even once.

The friends Alison brought had giggled with Matthew and Brent as the night wore on, but Mike was the odd man out, not wanting to flirt with some random chick and not knowing what to say to get into Kenley's good graces. Her cold shoulder made him feel unwelcome at his own damn SEAL team's night on the beach. How ironic was that?

Christopher chuckled. "Lexi kept asking if I thought you two hooked up again or something."

"You've got to be kidding me."

"Does that sound like Lexi?" Christopher smirked. "Not a chance in hell. But that little show you and Kenley put on by the pool was quite impressive."

Mike groaned. The memory of Kenley's lush body pressed against his was enough to fill his fantasies for an entire year. The way that bikini top stretched across her full breasts, leaving very little to the imagination. The way he'd rocked against her, feeling her heat even through her bikini bottoms. Hell, if they hadn't had an audience, he'd have taken her right then and there. Slipped that scrap of fabric to the side and thrust straight into heaven. He was dying to send Kenley soaring, to have her moaning and begging him for more.

"That good, huh?" Christopher asked.

"Fucking amazing," Mike admitted. He cleared his throat. "But as you could see last night, she's still pissed at me."

"About the condo?"

"Yeah, I don't think most women take strange men barging into their homes lightly."

"I told you to get the fuck off of her," Christopher pointed out.

"I did. But between that and tossing her into the pool? She's pissed. And how the hell was I supposed to know she doesn't swim?"

Christopher chuckled. "No woman who was furious at you would let you kiss her like that. She wants you too, man."

Mike shrugged. "It sure didn't seem that way last night."

Christopher walked over to answer the door, and a moment later, Patrick came in carrying two large pizzas and a six-pack.

"I know you said you already had beer, but I figured extra wouldn't hurt." His gaze swept the room. "Hell, this place is a goddamn mess."

"Nice of you to join us," Mike said, rolling his eyes.

Patrick dropped the boxes of pizza down on the coffee table and nailed him with gaze. "All right, Patch," Patrick said, calling Mike by his nickname. "What the hell was going on last night at the bonfire? First you run off, then Kenley runs off. Then she returns in your clothing but refuses to speak to you." He raised his eyebrows, his cool blue eyes assessing him.

"Jesus Christ," Mike muttered, walking over to grab a beer. "Not you, too."

"Rebecca was worried. She said Kenley was practically crying by the time you guys came back."

Shit. Mike's gut churned at the idea of Kenley being upset with him. Of the knowledge that he'd somehow hurt her. She was so small and fragile, he'd never do anything to cause her harm. Hell, he and the men on his team would never hurt any woman. And as for the brunette beauty he couldn't get out of his mind? Well, the fact that she'd been brought to tears because of something he did didn't sit well with him. At all. Part of him wanted to remedy the situation immediately—and another part of him wanted to stay the hell away. He couldn't cause her harm if he wasn't around.

He knew Kenley had been angry when he asked why she was frightened of him, but she sure the hell hadn't been crying on their walk back. She'd marched off in a huff, and they hadn't even spoken again. He felt like the biggest jerk in the world for making her feel bad. Again. Maybe he *should* just stay the hell away from her. Try as he might to do right by her, he seemed to just keep digging himself a deeper grave with every encounter—crash and burn.

Christopher tossed him a bottle opener, and Mike popped the cap on the bottle, taking a long pull of the cold brew. "I didn't know she was upset, Ice," Mike said. "Angry, yes. But crying?" He blew out a breath.

"I was just giving him the third degree," Christopher admitted, grabbing a beer for himself.

"You want one?" he asked, nodding at Patrick.

"Hell yeah. Thanks, man."

Mike took another swig of his beer as his two teammates stared at him. "Seriously? You two are turning into chicks or something. I should've spent the day with Matthew and Brent."

"They're probably still with the women they met last night," Patrick said with a laugh.

"Good God," Mike muttered.

"Is Rebecca with the kids today?" Christopher asked Patrick.

Rebecca had a young daughter who was four, and Patrick had a six-year-old son. They'd originally met when their kids were playing together. Those two had been hot and heavy from the start, and after an incident with a stalker chasing after Rebecca, they'd been practically inseparable ever since. Even though Christopher and Lexi were the first of the group to get engaged, Mike didn't doubt that Patrick would soon be following in his footsteps. Mike's weekends with the guys would probably be getting fewer and fewer. Hell.

"Yeah, they all went for ice cream on the boardwalk," Patrick said.

"Lexi and Kenley went to the spa for the day."

"Man, you are whipped," Mike said with a laugh. "Lexi gets to spend the day at the spa while you move furniture around all day?"

"You obviously know nothing about relationships," Christopher said.

"That is one thing I'll agree with you on. And it's better that way—trust me."

"I don't know. Kenley sure seems to get your motor running." Christopher waggled his eyebrows.

Patrick laughed. "You know what they say—the bigger they are, the harder they fall.

"I'm not falling for anything," Mike muttered.

Patrick and Christopher exchanged a glance. Mike didn't miss the smirk on Patrick's face. Hell. What was with those two today?

"That's what they all say," Christopher said with a grin. "Right up until they meet their dream girl. So tell me, have you had any dreams about Kenley?"

"Enough," Mike ground out as the other guys chuckled.

"All right," Christopher said, putting an end to the joking around. "Let's move the rest of the furniture in the living room and watch the game. We can deal with all the boxes for storage later on. Pizza's getting cold."

The three men moved enough things around to make room for when some of Lexi's furniture would eventually move in with her. The place didn't look half-bad, Mike thought. They'd probably get a bigger place soon, but it would work for the two of them in the meantime.

Mike collapsed on the sofa and knocked off a beer while they chowed down on pizza and watched the game. He'd gotten in ten miles this morning before heading over to help move furniture, and the cheese pizza tasted pretty damn spectacular with an ice cold one after all that exertion. The guys had some intense training on the water tomorrow, so he wouldn't overindulge. Mike and the rest of the SEAL team kept to a strict diet and training regimen to stay in shape. It worked pretty well judging from all the attention from the ladies. It sure felt good to kick back with pizza and beers rather than the MREs they were forced to eat on their deployments. As much as he loved the action, he'd take football and friends over their recent ops.

"Oh, I almost forget," Christopher said, grabbing a balled up sweatshirt and tossing it at Mike.

Mike snagged it from the air and looked at Christopher questioningly.

"Kenley came by earlier to pick up Lexi for their spa day."

Mike nodded and set the rumpled sweatshirt down beside him, a lump suddenly forming in his throat. She'd been here, and he'd managed to miss her. He hoped like hell he'd get a chance to talk to her whenever the girls got back. This nonsense was eating him up inside. And the fact that Kenley had been crying last night? Damn it. Even if nothing ever did happen between them, if that kiss had been a onetime only deal, he needed to make things right.

He turned his attention back to the game, trying to focus on the action. Christopher and Patrick cheered loudly a minute later, and Mike blinked, having missed the entire play. The scent of vanilla wafted up to him, and he groaned. Hell. His sweatshirt even smelled like Kenley. He was such a goner.

Chapter 6

Kenley dreamily closed her eyes as the masseuse adjusted the warm towel and began massaging her shoulders and upper back. The firm strokes kneaded her aching muscles, and she happily gave in to a moment of pure bliss. The scent of lavender and other essential oils permeated the air, soothing music filled the dim room, and she felt so relaxed that if she let herself, she could drift off to sleep.

"You have some tension in your shoulders," the woman said.

"Mmm-hmm," Kenley mumbled. Tension indeed. She hadn't slept well at all last night, anger coursing through her from the encounter with Mike at the bonfire. What had he wanted on their walk back? For a moment, when he'd stepped right up to her, it had almost seemed like he was going to kiss her or something. Like he had a reason to after their little afternoon at the pool.

She didn't even like him. Jackass.

She'd carelessly tossed his sweatshirt onto the chair beside her bed last night, and that had been a mistake, because his spicy scent had filled her bedroom. His image had filled her dreams. His body had been moving over hers, the scruff from his five o'clock shadow scraping against her skin, his hardened cock rubbing her just where she needed him…and she'd woken up. Flushed and aroused and angry all at the same time. Not to mention unsatisfied. She'd tossed and turned after that, unwilling to let herself waste another minute thinking of him. Unwilling to spend another *second* on that insufferable man.

And the fact that she'd actually been turned on by her dreams of him? Well that was just the last straw. She was done associating with Mike. The sooner she finished up this project and made it back to the safety of her apartment in Northern Virginia, the better. Lexi could have Christopher and the guys on his SEAL team, because Kenley sure the hell didn't want anything to do with any of them. She'd find a nice, boring guy to settle down with and move on. End of discussion.

"Think the guys are done moving everything around the apartment?" Lexi asked sleepily from the adjacent massage table.

Kenley opened one eye and looked over at her blissed-out friend. Lexi's eyes were shut, her jet black hair cascading down one side, and Kenley was happy they had a girl's day to relax and unwind. After the kidnapping incident a few weeks ago, Lexi deserved a day to not worry about a thing. It had been tough on her at first to be alone, but between Christopher's reappearance in her life and Kenley's temporary assignment in town, the two of them had kept her occupied and helped her readjust.

Their spa day had been in the works for two weeks. Kenley was glad they'd finally coordinated their schedules to spend the day being pampered. First they'd had facials, then they'd relaxed in the heat of the sauna. After their hour-long massages, they'd get mani-pedis and enjoy a late lunch. Perfect way to spend a Sunday.

"Probably. Christopher will do anything you ask him to." The man was completely smitten with Lexi, and Kenley was happy they'd rekindled their decade-old romance and gotten engaged. Her best friend deserved nothing but happiness. It was ironic that the man Lexi had hated the most had been the one she'd ended up with, but life was funny sometimes. The way Kenley's own life was going, she didn't imagine herself ending up with *anyone*. But she was thrilled for Lexi.

Kenley groaned as the masseuse massaged her instep, and she heard Lexi's soft laughter in the background.

"I'm sure Mike would do anything you asked him to," Lexi teased.

"Oh God. No more talk about Mike."

"I only said one thing!" Lexi protested.

"One thing too many."

"You were pretty upset last night when you got back to the bonfire. If the situation with Mike is bothering you that much, don't you think it means something?"

"Nope. Doesn't mean a damn thing."

Lexi snorted in disagreement, and Kenley closed

her eyes again.

"He's over there now you know."

"Who is?" Kenley asked as she flipped over, letting the masseuse work on her temples and scalp.

"Mike."

Kenley instantly froze. "What?"

"Relax," the masseuse chastised. Kenley squeezed her eyes shut, but her heart beat furiously in her chest. Blood pounded through her veins. She took a deep breath and tried to calm down, focusing on the soothing music in the background. Couldn't she even enjoy her Sunday without dealing with this drama?

"He's helping Christopher move furniture around. They're making room for when I move in."

"Perfect," Kenley groaned. "At least he'll be gone by the time we got back."

Lexi laughed. "Not likely. They're watching the game. You'll see him when we get back. Unless you just drop me off without coming inside and run off like a scaredy-cat."

"Then that's the plan," Kenley agreed.

"Oh come on," Lexi protested. "You can't leave me alone with a bunch of men watching football."

"Not even when one of them is your fiancé?" Kenley commented dryly.

"Besides, I'm pretty sure Mike has a thing for you. That kiss at the pool looked pretty scorching hot. And he didn't stop looking at you once last night."

"Oh, give it a rest. I'll be going back to Northern Virginia soon anyway, and Mike will be ancient history."

"Famous last words."

Thirty minutes later the two women were showered, dressed, and relaxing with their feet in bubbling foot spas as they got prepped for their pedicures. Kenley handed the dark polish she'd selected to the attendant, the dull color suiting her mood. She'd been having a perfectly relaxing day until Mike's name had been mentioned. Ugh. Why did he stress her out so much? Why was she still even thinking about him?

"So how've you been after everything?" Kenley asked. "Any more nightmares?"

The kidnapping a few weeks ago had left Lexi shaken. She'd confided in Kenley that she'd had trouble sleeping, but she'd all but moved in with Christopher for the time being. Kenley was relieved Lexi had him. The Defense Department had granted Lexi a month of leave to deal with her trauma, so she hadn't even returned to work yet. Although Lexi was hoping to relocate to Virginia Beach, she'd be returning to Arlington and her job at the Pentagon soon, just as Kenley would be returning to her home office up there. It would be surreal to go back and return to her old routine, but life moved on.

"I have good days and bad days. Mostly good—I mean thank God nothing happened when I was kidnapped. I was scared, but it's not like they actually hurt me. I just still don't like being alone."

"I understand. You should stay with me when we go back to Arlington."

"Yeah?"

"Absolutely. We can be roomies for a while."

"I'd like that. Christopher's not too happy that I'll be leaving soon."

Kenley shrugged. "I get why he's overprotective, but you have your work there, and he's got his SEAL team here. It's not like either of you can just pick up and immediately move. Think you'll get the job down at Little Creek?"

"It seems likely," Lexi said. "They need someone who's an IT expert—"

"And that just happens to be your specialty," Kenley laughed. "Well, that's pretty damn perfect then. I wish you never had to go through the kidnapping, but it sounds like everything will work out for the best."

"You're right. I never imagined I'd even see Christopher again after ten years—let alone somehow end up working with him and getting engaged. You just never know where life will take you."

The nail technician spread peppermint foot scrub all over Kenley's feet and calves, and she happily sighed. Too bad she couldn't justify getting pampered like this every weekend.

"This feels heavenly," Lexi said.

"I was just thinking the same."

"We should do a girl's spa day before the wedding. You, me, and Cassidy," she said, referring to the third women in their trio of friends. Cassidy had come down for a weekend to visit with them but had to return home to work. She'd taken one look at all the hunky military men wandering around town and had promised to return soon, Kenley remembered with a smile.

"That sounds perfect. And one of these weekends we need to go dress shopping!"

"Absolutely. You'll be my maid of honor, right?"

"Of course!" Kenley said, beaming.

The women relaxed and chatted as they finished up at the spa. After their mani-pedis had dried, they decided to go to a seafood restaurant down by the water for a late lunch. Kenley found a parking spot on the busy street, just down the block from one of their favorite places to eat, and the two women walked around the corner. The area was crowded with locals and vacationers enjoying a relaxing Sunday afternoon down by the ocean. Hopefully they could nab a spot on the outdoor patio, enjoying some of the warmth of the late October day.

Kenley's stomach rumbled as she smelled the delicious aroma of food permeating the air. It had been way too long since breakfast that morning. She was already planning exactly what to order when a car door slammed, and Lexi stiffened beside her. A man in a dark suit and sunglasses got out of a blacked-out SUV across the street. Nothing seemed out of the ordinary, but as Kenley continued to walk down the sidewalk, she noticed Lexi was frozen in place.

"Lexi? Everything okay?" Kenley asked, growing concerned.

"That looks like him," Lexi said frantically.

"Looks like who? OH!" Kenley exclaimed, suddenly realizing Lexi had mistaken the man in the SUV for the asshole who'd kidnapped her. "Lexi, that bastard is in jail. That's not him," she said soothingly, grabbing onto Lexi's arm.

Lexi began to tremble, and Kenley pulled her friend into a souvenir shop off the main drag. They still hadn't gotten lunch, but they couldn't exactly continue to the restaurant given Lexi's current state. "What do you want to do? We can leave," Kenley assured her. "You want to wait here while I get the car? Or we can walk back together."

"No, I can't go back outside," Lexi said, shaking.

"Sweetie, it's not him," Kenley soothed. "Want me

to call Christopher?"

"Yeah," Lexi said, eyes watering.

Kenley pulled her cell phone from her purse and selected Christopher's home number from her contact list. It went straight to voicemail, so she tried again. If the guys were at the apartment moving stuff around and watching football for hours, why hadn't he picked up?

"Hello?" a deep voice answered after two more rings.

"Christopher?"

"No, this is Mike. Lexi?"

"Kenley."

"Is everything okay?" Mike asked, sounding concerned.

"Well, yes and no. Lexi's freaking out because she saw a man that looked like her kidnapper. Obviously it's not him, but I don't know what to do. We're in a store, and she doesn't want to go back outside. I think maybe she's having a panic attack or something. Is Christopher there?"

"No, they're dropping off stuff in storage. Where are you?"

Kenley gave him the name and location of the shop. It wasn't too far down the street from Anchors, the bar the guys on the SEAL team liked to frequent. Christopher should be able to find them easily once they got hold of him. She glanced back at Lexi, who was suddenly looking wan.

"Lexi looks really pale. Maybe I should take her to the doctor or something. Or the emergency room."

"Have she eaten anything?"

"No, we were just on our way to lunch."

"She might be in shock. Get her some juice or

something if you can to raise her blood sugar. I'll be there in ten minutes."

"Juice, got it." She scanned the store, wondering if they even sold anything like that here.

"Kenley, hang tight. I'll be right there."

"But what about Christopher—"

"I'll be there in ten."

Kenley sighed as the call disconnected. The last person she wanted to see was Mike, but what was she supposed to do? Lexi was freaking out. She didn't want to drag her back outside in the midst of a full-blown panic attack. And she had to admit, she knew Lexi would feel better if one of the guys was there to offer protection. Although Kenley knew there was no threat, if it would ease her friend's mind to have Christopher or one of his SEAL buddies there, they might as well wait for Mike.

"I feel sort of dizzy," Lexi said weakly.

Kenley looked around the store again and saw a refrigerated beverages section near the back. Grabbing an apple juice, she made her way to the front and paid for it, instructing Lexi to take a few sips.

"Is everything okay?" the young cashier asked.

"Yeah, she just saw someone outside that freaked her out."

"Her ex?" the cashier asked, snapping her gum. "Because my ex is a jackass. Want me to call the cops?"

"No, we're fine," Kenley said, scanning the street. A moment later Mike came rushing in, looking muscular and mouth-watering in cargo khaki pants and a football jersey. His large frame filled the entire doorway, and the cashier gasped in shock at his larger than life presence. He looked ready to take on the world and fight off anything that would harm them.

"Is that him? I can call the police."

"No, he's fine. That's our friend," Kenley said as Mike approached. Friend? Well he wouldn't hurt them in any case, which is what the cashier seemed concerned about. And it's not like he was a random stranger off the street.

Mike raised his eyebrows without comment and immediately grabbed Lexi's wrist, taking her pulse. Kenley knew that all of the guys on the SEAL team had some medical training, out of necessity, but she imagined that was more for life or death situations in battle, not women going into shock. She imagined him stopping profuse bleeding and applying tourniquets to injured men, maybe even slinging some guy over his shoulder and running to a waiting helicopter. But rushing into stores and assisting distraught women? Not exactly.

Mike eyed his watch as he waited and seemed to be timing her pulse. Nodding with satisfaction when he was finished, he ducked lower to look into Lexi's eyes. "Lexi, are you okay, sweetheart?" he asked.

An unexpected surge of jealousy washed over Kenley at Mike's term of endearment. He was just being nice to her; obviously they all knew she was with Christopher. So what was with her instant resentment? He was here to help her best friend. Kenley suddenly had an odd longing to know what Mike would call her in a situation like that. Sweetheart? Baby? Something else entirely?

Lexi nodded, her violet eyes watery.

"I called Christopher, and he's on his way back right now," Mike continued. "I'll drive you both back to his apartment."

"But that guy—"

"Wasn't the kidnapper," Mike finished. "I know you're frightened, but that wasn't him."

"Are you okay to leave?" Kenley asked. "Let's forget the restaurant. We'll pick up some food on the way home."

"Yeah. I just want to get out of here."

Mike put his arm around Lexi's shoulders and guided her to the front door, glancing back over his shoulder to make sure Kenley was with them. Her heart pounded furiously as his blue gaze met hers. He hadn't bothered to shave this morning, and the scruff on his jaw made him look harder than ever. Not to mention hotter than hell.

Kenley had to admit that she liked how he controlled the situation. He'd come to get them, helped Lexi, made sure Kenley was taken care of as well. She still had no idea why Christopher hadn't rushed over himself, even if he had been putting boxes in storage, but she could respect the fact that his SEAL team looked out for one another. It hadn't even been a question if Mike would come help them—he'd just immediately said he'd be there, and he was.

They exited the store, and once on the sidewalk, Kenley gestured the other way. "I parked down there."

"I'll drive us all back together," Mike said. "I can drop you at your car later on."

"Oh, I can just—"

Mike nailed her with a gaze, tilting his head toward Lexi, who still looked really shaken up. Maybe it would be best if she rode with them. It would probably help calm Lexi down. But that meant she'd have to be alone in the car with Mike later on. Hopefully World War III wouldn't erupt when they were left alone together. Still, he was being nothing but a perfect gentleman right now.

"Yeah, let's do it," she agreed.

They walked down the block to Mike's large black SUV, and Mike helped Lexi into the passenger seat. Kenley watched as he fastened her seatbelt, and she felt a sudden surge of warmth wash over her. As aggressive as Mike and the rest of those guys were, they also seemed to have a caring side. A need to protect and care for others. Mike had rushed over here at a moment's notice to help her and Lexi. How could she begrudge someone as selfless as that?

"She probably needs some food," Kenley said as Mike shut the door.

"Agreed. We'll pick up something on the way back."

"All right." She turned to get into the backseat of the SUV, and Mike's large hand came to a rest on the small of her back, guiding her. His searing touch burned into her skin like a bolt of lightning and sent heat and awareness surging through her body. Even when he removed his hand to open the door for her, she felt the imprint of it there, like he'd marked her.

She climbed in and tucked her legs into the back of the vehicle but didn't miss the flash of interest in Mike's eyes as she glanced up at him. He simply nodded and shut the door, but the expression on his face sent lust and longing racing through her system. Maybe he had simply been trying to do the right thing all those weeks ago when he'd scared her out of her mind. *Maybe.* Still. They'd go back to the apartment, he'd give her a ride to get her car, and that would be that. No sense on dwelling on these crazy feelings she was suddenly having. Or imagining part two of their kiss at the pool.

"Where was this guy anyway?" he asked as he climbed into the driver's seat.

"That SUV right over there," Kenley said, pointing across the street.

Mike gripped the steering wheel, his gaze focused on the black SUV just down the block. His spicy scent filled the interior of the vehicle, and Kenley nervously swallowed. He sat so large, looming right in front of her. But she felt safe. Sheltered. Even though logically she knew the man they'd seen wasn't Lexi's kidnapper, who was behind bars, she had to admit that it felt good to have someone take care of them. To take care of her. Her own parents were never around, and this man she barely knew, who was friends with Lexi's fiancé, had rushed to their aid without a second thought. How ironic since her own family didn't seem to see things that way.

"I know I freaked out over nothing, but I swear it looked just like him," Lexi said.

"That asshole is behind bars," Mike said, swinging his glance over to her. "But I swear to God, Lexi, none of us will let anything happen to you again. If you're ever frightened, and Christopher's not around, you can give any of us a call. We'll be there immediately."

Mike pulled his cell phone from his pocket. "What's your cell number?" he asked Lexi.

She recited it, and Mike punched it in and sent her a text. "Now you have my number. Save it in your contact list," he instructed. "Kenley, tell me your number, too."

Startled, Kenley recited her cell number. She felt strangely excited about Mike knowing how to reach her. Obviously he wanted it for safety measures—for emergencies. But the thought that he could now call her at any time had her heart racing. She tucked her phone back into her purse after she added Mike to her contacts, telling herself she was being silly. If something happened and they needed help, it made sense to be able to contact some of the guys. That was all this was about.

Mike started the engine and pulled into the street, heading the opposite way of her car and the restaurant and toward Christopher's apartment. His heated blue gaze met hers in the rearview mirror, and she shifted uncomfortably in her seat. Maybe riding alone with him wasn't such a good idea—at the moment, she had the craziest desire to give in to her urges. To pull him close and kiss him, inhaling all of his soap and spice. To give in to whatever he wanted, letting him command and control her body as easily as he had yesterday. To allow him just one night.

She swallowed nervously, immediately quashing that idea. Mike was being nice now, yes, but that didn't mean he wouldn't act like a jerk again when the mood struck. His cocky, holier-than-thou attitude wasn't something she needed or wanted. His rush off to save the world lifestyle wasn't something that would offer her any safety or stability. She'd lived that life as a kid, having family that was never around, and when she did eventually find a man she wanted to spend her life with, he'd be there for her one hundred percent of the time. No questions asked.

She glanced out the window, watching the

restaurants and hotels go by. She wouldn't even be in town much longer to pursue something if she'd wanted to. She'd go her way, and Mike would go his. Life moved on, and a guy like him would never be a permanent fixture in hers.

Chapter 7

"Is she okay?" Patrick asked half an hour later, his brow furrowing.

They'd all gathered back in Christopher's apartment, and Mike glanced over to where Lexi stood in the kitchen with Kenley and Christopher. They each had an arm around her, and Christopher was rubbing her back in a soothing motion. "Yeah, I think she just got spooked. They saw some guy that looked like the jackass who kidnapped her."

Patrick stiffened and clenched his fists. "That shit is messed up. I wish they would've let us deal with him our own way; I would've beaten that son of a bitch within an inch of his life."

Mike nodded grimly. "Not if Christopher had anything to say about it. He would've killed him with his bare hands."

"There's something fucked up about guys who harm women and children. I swear to God, if anything had happened to Rebecca when that stalker was after her, I never would've been able to live with myself."

"I hear you," Mike said, glancing over at Kenley again. She looked petite and fragile in the short, loose dress she had on. It skimmed her curves and left plenty to the imagination, but there was something sexy as hell about it. A lightweight cardigan covered her slender arms, but those gorgeous bare legs were on full display again.

When the weather turned cooler in a few weeks, he was going to miss all the peeks of skin. Those shorts from the other night, this dress…. Hell, especially that killer bikini she'd had on. What he wouldn't give to spend a night exploring all of her womanly curves. Kissing every inch of her body. Finding out what she liked, what made her cry out his name. His groin tightened, and she glanced over his way, almost as if she knew he was watching her.

A cascade of brown curls framed her delicate face, and her cheeks flushed slightly when she met his gaze. He barely knew the woman, but somehow he felt protective toward her. Possessive. He didn't want her to return to Arlington and fall into the arms of another man—he wanted her here. Now. In his arms and in his bed. Hell, if no one else had been around, he had half a mind to march over there, pull her into his arms, and kiss her until they both admitted there was something brewing between them. That it hadn't just been one intense kiss yesterday that had them both stirred up.

Mike and all the men on his SEAL team had been trained to read people—and even if she was throwing up walls like she was building a damn fortress, he was certain she was interested. He'd seen the way she looked at him. Felt the ways her eyes caressed his body when she thought he was unaware. And there was no hiding her excitement when he'd kissed her yesterday in the pool. Those little gasps and pants along with the desperate way she clung to him gave him half a mind to chase after her and never let her go.

The fact that she wanted him too made him harder than hell. What would it take to convince her to give in to temptation once more? To prove that yesterday hadn't been a mistake and that he deserved a chance?

"Christopher just about lost his shit when you called us," Patrick said.

"I can imagine. Is there more stuff to move or are we all set for the day?"

"We moved all the boxes to the storage unit, so we're good. I'll probably head out if things are under control. We've got training early tomorrow, and I want to spend some time with the kids."

"Kids, huh?" Mike asked with a smirk.

"Don't knock it 'til you've tried it," Patrick said, punching him in the arm.

"Thanks again guys for helping today," Christopher said, walking over. "I think Lexi just needs some time alone now."

"Yeah, we're gonna head out," Mike said. "Unless you need help with anything else."

"I think we're set," Christopher said. "Sorry about missing the end of the game."

"Don't sweat it," Patrick said. "Family comes first."

"I guess I should get going, too," Kenley said as she joined them. Mike's gaze flicked back to the kitchen, where Lexi had sunk down into a chair and was sipping some tea, looking completely exhausted.

"I'll drop you back at your car," Mike said, meeting Kenley's gaze. She nodded uncertainly, and his gut clenched. Hell, was she afraid to be alone with him? What was it going to take to convince her he was a decent guy? Staying the hell away from her was seeming like less and less of an option.

Patrick glanced between the two of them, noticing the tension. "I can drop you off if you like," he said.

"Um, thanks, but I'm okay. I can get a ride with Mike."

Patrick raised his eyebrows, and Mike felt a swell of male pride surging through his chest. Even if Kenley was uncertain, the fact that she'd just agreed to be alone with him had to be a good sign.

"Then let's get going. Should we say goodbye to Lexi?"

"No," Christopher said. "Just let her rest. I'll see you guys tomorrow."

They exchanged goodbyes, and then Mike, Patrick, and Kenley walked outside to the parking lot. Mike clicked the remote to his SUV and opened the passenger door for Kenley. He tried not to groan as she ducked into the vehicle. Hell. That dress was getting his imagination all sorts of worked up. What he wouldn't give to bend her over the nearest surface, flip up that flimsy little dress, and sink straight into heaven.

No doubt that would freak her the hell out, he thought with a smirk. He could be patient. Mike had the distinct impression that Kenley would be well worth the wait. He was impressed with the way she'd handled herself during the few weeks he'd known her.

She'd rushed down from Northern Virginia when her best friend was in trouble. She'd handled him after he'd eventually released her at the condo. Maybe physically she hadn't been able to fend him off when he thought she was one of the kidnappers, but verbally? Damn. She'd given him a tongue lashing he'd never forget once she'd gotten her wits about her.

And she was sweet. Sensitive. All her soft curves up against his male hardness was just about damn near perfection. Her body fit against his she'd been made just for him and him alone. And what he wouldn't give to learn all the other ways their bodies perfectly aligned—to sweep his tongue inside her sweet mouth. To bury his cock so deep inside her tight walls that neither of them knew where he stopped and she began. To thrust into her again and again, driving her skyward until she screamed out his name.

Hell. He had to get his mind off getting her into his bed and onto driving her back. His pants had already grown uncomfortably tight.

"You didn't eat much," Mike said as he eased into the driver's seat. "Want me to take you to get some food?"

"Oh. I was just worried about Lexi, I guess."

He started the engine and glanced over at her. "It's normal to have some trauma after a situation like that. It'll take her a while to get readjusted, but she's actually doing great."

"You seem pretty confident," Kenley commented.

Mike shrugged. He glanced back over his shoulder and backed out of the space. Patrick was already pulling out onto the road. "I've had medical training.

We have to know how to treat men who are in shock if they're injured in battle."

"Do all the guys have medical training?"

"Yeah, to some extent. Theirs is more basic though. Every man on the team has to have a particular skill set—Christopher's the IT guru, as you probably already know. Patrick is our team leader. I'm the medic in the group. That's how I got my nickname."

"Patch, right?"

"Yeah, because I patch people up."

Kenley laughed, and a sudden feeling of warmth filled his chest. She sure didn't laugh much around him, and hell if he didn't wish that wasn't the case. Her whole face lit up when she smiled, and her eyes shone brightly. Not to mention that rosy hue that crossed her cheeks, which is what Mike liked to imagine she might look like when she came—panting and screaming his name in ecstasy.

"When did you get that nickname?"

"Not until my first op. Some guys get theirs in BUD/S—that's the training we have to do to become a SEAL. But I was, uh, attending to a guy who'd gotten a bullet wound in the leg. He was ready to keep on fighting and was screaming at me to patch him up so he could get back into battle."

"Was it one of the guys on your SEAL team now?"

"No, I was originally with a different unit. This one's the best though."

He glanced over to see Kenley smirking. "Modest as always, I see."

Mike chuffed out a laugh. "Hey, I'll admit I can be cocky some of the time—hell, maybe even a lot of the time. But when it comes to my guys, I'm not just blowing smoke up your ass. Uh, sorry. I just mean we're the best of the best. Not even a question."

Mike pulled onto the road that made up the main drag of Virginia Beach. It was dotted with hotels, restaurants, and souvenir shops. Not to mention plenty of tourists and locals who'd been enjoying a lazy Sunday down by the water. "So listen, I know we got off to a bad start a few weeks ago. And with the whole jumping into the pool thing yesterday. Let me buy you dinner—make up for it."

"Dinner?"

"Yeah, that meal people eat at the end of the day."

"I know what dinner is," Kenley said, rolling her eyes. "I just don't know why you think us going to dinner together is a good idea."

"It's an apology. And it's just dinner—I promise I won't make any moves on you."

Kenley blushed as Mike raised his eyebrows. It was too damn easy to get a rise out of her. The ways she reacted to everything he said was priceless. "That is, unless you want me to. I sure didn't mind kissing you in the pool." He winked, watching her turn an even deeper shade of red. Hell yeah, this was going to be a good night.

Chapter 8

Mike eased into a parking spot on the busy road, instructing Kenley to sit tight until he could help her out of the SUV. She watched him round the front of the vehicle and felt a small flush of pleasure at his attentiveness. Was this how he treated all the women in his life that he was supposedly only friends with? Unlikely. And who was she kidding—they weren't exactly "just friends." Not with the heated glances he'd been throwing at her for the past hour. She could pretend all she wanted, but after that kiss they'd shared at the pool? She wasn't fooling anyone. Not even herself.

He opened the door, and her breath caught as he reached out to help her. Kenley let Mike take her hand and help her out of his SUV, his large, muscular hand nearly enveloping her much smaller one. His grip was warm and firm, and she tried not to gasp at his closeness. At the heat she could feel from his large frame as he hovered over her. His other hand came to a rest atop the open door, essentially trapping her against the passenger seat.

She tilted her head back, meeting his eyes.

"I like you," he said, his voice husky.

Heat coursed over her skin. "Excuse me?" She couldn't have heard him correctly. Hadn't he just said a few minutes ago he wasn't going to pull anything?

He ducked his head lower, holding her gaze. "I like you. I don't play games; I don't beat around the bush. I'll be your friend, but know that I want more." His thumb lightly caressed her knuckles, sending shivers down her spine, and then he released her, backing away, giving her space. Leaving far too much distance between them again.

She didn't know how to react to that. Maybe there was some sort of electricity still sparking between them, but she was leaving in another week or so. And he was all wrong for her. She didn't do one-night-stands; she didn't need a guy like him around. Except—no one else had made her feel so alive in such a short amount of time. They'd only spent the briefest of moments together, and each time it hadn't been nearly long enough. Her body craved more of everything—his touch, his voice, his scent. The unfinished promise of what could happen between them if only she'd let it.

It didn't mean anything though. She was in lust, maybe, but not in the beginnings of a relationship. That kiss yesterday might've been the best kiss she'd ever had, but it had been a fantasy. A moment of adrenaline and heightened hormones. And since she'd be gone in days, not a thing would ever come of it.

Shakily she stepped onto the sidewalk as Mike shut

the door, setting the alarm. "Where to?" he asked, acting as if nothing out of the ordinary had happened.

She felt off-kilter by his admission but steeled herself, determined to pretend everything was fine. "Do you like seafood?"

"Angel, I'm in the Navy. I'll eat anything."

Did he just call her…angel? She hastened a glance his way, and he winked.

Brushing it aside, she began walking. "Lexi and I were planning to eat at this seafood place down the block. Does that sound good?"

"Sure, wherever you want is good with me."

"Did you guys get to finish helping Christopher today before everything happened?"

"Yeah, we moved a ton of furniture around as you could probably tell. And Patrick and Christopher hauled a bunch of things down to storage. It's all set for whenever Lexi wants to move in."

"Wow. It'll be so strange when she's down here permanently."

"You can come visit; it's just a few hours away. I'll even let you stay with me if you want." He casually slung his arm around her shoulder, and she sighed. His warmth and strength beside her felt too good. Maybe he was claiming to be playing it casual, but her body was screaming for more of those heated kisses and stolen caresses.

"Are you forgetting my parents have a condo here?" she asked lightly.

"Ah, the infamous condo. I couldn't forget that—that's where we first met."

"Met," she scoffed. "You held me against the wall when you thought I was one of the kidnappers."

Mike ducked his head low, his lips hovering near

her ear. "The next time I have you against a wall, it will be for an entirely different reason."

She flushed, heat coursing through her veins, as images of Mike holding her against him flashed through her mind. There were a few different ways to interpret that statement, all of them entirely too tempting. All of them entirely wrong for her.

His lips brushed against her cheek, heating her skin even more. "I love how you blush around me, Kenley. It makes me think you're more affected by me than you want to admit."

Embarrassed, Kenley abruptly pulled away from him, putting her hands on her hips. "What do you want Mike? You acted like this was just a friendly dinner, but obviously it's not."

He raised his eyebrows, a smug expression crossing his face. "I wanted to see how you'd react. You sure seemed to like me yesterday at the pool. Then at the bonfire, you blew me off. So which is it?"

Kenley threw her arms up in the air. "I give up. Forget about dinner. I've got to go."

"Kenley, wait—" he said, gently grabbing her arm as she turned to leave. "I'm sorry." His fingers barely clasped her arm, but she felt trapped in place, tethered to him. She took a deep breath, desperately trying to fill her lungs with precious oxygen. Why was it so hard to breathe around him? It was like he sucked all the air from the space around her, leaving her breathless. Making her desperate to stop whatever it was he did to her—before she fell so hard there was no turning back.

"We'll never be friends, Mike," she said angrily. "We'll never be anything."

His expression clouded, and a hint of regret

flashed across his eyes. "Kenley, I'm sorry."

"Yeah, sorry you're acting like a jackass. But what's the point? You'll act nice for a little while then turn into a jerk again.'

"Let me walk you back to your car."

"Don't bother," she said, stalking away. Knowing he would follow, she glanced back over her shoulder and shot him an icy glare. "Just leave me the hell alone."

**

Mike watched Kenley walk away and muttered a curse.

He'd pushed her too far after promising he wouldn't hit on her tonight. But hell, how long she going to go around acting like there was nothing between them? He'd kissed plenty of women over the years, but that kiss he and Kenley had shared yesterday? It had been the hottest one of his life. Holding her to him in the pool like that, feeling all of her softness up against him, the sweet and gentle way she'd yielded to his kiss and touch? It made him want a hell of a lot more time alone with her.

He didn't think a little harmless flirting would cause her to freak out like that. He was a man, not some teenage boy too shy to talk to the pretty girls. If he was interested in a woman, he'd let her know. What was there to pretend about anyway? They were consenting adults. Maybe he did want to take her to dinner and then straight to his bed, but that didn't mean the night would've ended that way.

He sighed, looking back and forth on the busy road. He still needed to eat, and they had early training tomorrow. His phone buzzed, and he pulled it out of his pocket to see a text from Brent. He and Matthew were at Anchors tonight. Might as well join them, he supposed. He had to eat sometime, and Kenley had just blown him off. He sure the hell would've liked her company more than his buddies, but what was he supposed to do? Chase her down the street like some asshole? She clearly didn't want to see him.

Walking down the block, he pushed open the door to the busy bar. Even on a Sunday evening it was packed, and Mike scanned the room. A group of women near him made a big show of giving him the once over, but he didn't give them a second glance. His buddies were at a table in the back, along with a couple of co-eds who were laughing hysterically at whatever Brent was saying. Mike noted the women they were with were not the nurses from last night. Hell. Wouldn't those guys ever tire of an endless parade of women? Maybe he was getting too old for this scene.

He'd left Christopher and Lexi at their place; Patrick had been hurrying home to see Rebecca and their kids. Even Evan, the youngest man on their SEAL team, now had a girlfriend. He and Alison lived together and seemed completely content. Although Mike usually enjoyed weekend nights out with his buddies, the women and booze a welcome relief from the stress of their training and deployments, the days were starting to feel a little empty.

Lately, he felt like he needed something more. Regret weighed on his chest from the way the evening had ended with Kenley and the dinner that never was. She hadn't even let him escort her back to her car, and that didn't sit well with him. Sure, she was a grown woman and could take care of herself, but that didn't mean he wouldn't safely see her to where she was going.

He nodded to the waitress for a beer as he crossed the bar and then grabbed an empty seat at the table. The woman Brent had been talking to was now perched on his lap.

"Sure, I'd love to see those babies," he laughed as she pushed out her ample chest.

"I'd love to show you," she cooed.

Jesus. Could the woman be any more obvious? There was something entirely unappealing about women who came on too strong. Subtlety could work just fine, even for guys like them. Why didn't she just strip in front of Brent and show him her goods right now? Hell.

"Who's your friend?" the dark-haired beauty beside Matthew asked, coyly batting her lashes at him. She had on way too much make-up and a skintight top that left nothing to the imagination. Hell, he could probably guess her bra size in that thing.

"Are you deserting me already, darlin'?" Matthew asked, winking. The brunette laughed and appeared to be in no hurry to leave his side.

"Just weighing my options," she teased, licking her lips suggestively. She leaned against the table, putting her ample cleavage on display. Even Brent's attention flicked over.

"What's your name?" she asked Mike, sending him a mega-watt smile.

Good God. Although her rack was a sight to behold, it had to be fake. There was nothing attractive about that. Mike's mind flashed back to the sundress

Kenley had on today—it skimmed over her curves just so, giving him a hint of what lay beneath but leaving plenty to the imagination.

And hell if his imagination hadn't been working overtime.

He'd felt all her softness against him and knew she would be gorgeous. The rosiness of her lips was natural, not from some fancy, over-applied red lipstick. Would her nipples be that same rosy hue? He hardened just thinking about those full breasts of hers. He was dying to kiss and caress her, tasting, sucking her nipples into his mouth as he teased her. There was nothing he wanted more than Kenley crying out his name, begging him for more.

And after the abrupt dismissal she'd given him tonight? Hell, it made him want to chase after her even more. Even if she was uncertain around him at times, she wasn't afraid to stand up to him or tell him off when necessary. She sure the hell didn't throw herself at him like these overdone girls. And wasn't that a refreshing change.

"Don't worry about him," Matthew said, wrapping his arm around her shoulder. "Can I buy you another drink?"

"Maybe," she giggled. "If you ask nicely."

Mike resisted the urge to roll his eyes.

A loud raucous drew their attention from across the bar as two guys began arguing and shoving one another, a chair crashing to the floor. As one of the men stumbled backward, a woman behind him fell to the ground, caught in the melee. Her head connected with the edge of the table, which toppled over as well, sending plates, glasses, and bottles flying.

Mike, Matthew, and Brent rose instantly, hurrying

toward the commotion. Matthew helped the woman up as several bystanders looked on. Brent grabbed hold of the guy throwing punches, fire in his eyes.

"Enough!" he roared.

The man struggled, but Brent had him down on the ground in an instant.

"Get some ice for her!" Mike called out to one of the bartenders as he noticed the thin line of blood trailing down the woman's temple. He grabbed a clean napkin from a nearby table, tossing it to Matthew. "You two, out of here," he growled at the men, gesturing toward the door.

"Who the hell are you!" the man still standing shouted.

Anger coursed through Mike as he stepped closer, adrenaline surging through his veins. "Get the fuck out of here now, before we throw you out."

Brent yanked the guy on the ground up, causing him to wince in pain.

"Let's just go," the guy muttered.

The manager hurried over, checking to see how badly the woman was injured. "The police are on their way," he said to Mike and his teammates. "These two were in here causing trouble last week."

"They sure the hell won't be here again," Mike assured him, eyes blazing.

Sirens sounded in the distance, and the women they'd left at the table in the back waved goodbye and rushed out the front door. He and Matthew exchanged glances. "Underage?" Matthew questioned.

Hell. The women were in college but possibly not even twenty-one yet. Mike felt like an old man at thirty-two. He was too old to be playing these games in crowded bars with college girls. That's all they were—girls. He wasn't sure how old Kenley was, but she was definitely a woman. She had a job. A degree. Her own life. She sure didn't throw herself at him, wanting only to bed a Navy SEAL. Hell, if anything, she pulled away from him.

A few guys he recognized from base restrained the men as the police rushed in the door, and Mike knelt down to the injured woman. Matthew handed him a flashlight. He had no idea where he'd gotten one and didn't ask.

"Look at me," Mike instructed, aiming the light at the woman's pupils. She held the napkin to her temple, but fortunately, there didn't seem to be too much blood. A few minutes later the EMTs rushed in as the police were handcuffing the suspects. Mike turned the woman over to them, rejoining his friends.

"Those assholes need to learn to hold their liquor," Brent muttered. "That woman was hurt because of them."

"She'll be fine," Mike assured Brent. "Small cut to the temple, no signs of concussion."

Brent clenched his fists. "It makes me madder than hell to see dicks like them around. They didn't even give a shit as to all the women standing right there."

"I don't think they'll be coming back anytime soon," Matthew said dryly.

Mike nodded grimly as they watched the policemen lead the two men away in handcuffs. The workers at Anchors began cleaning up the food and drinks that spilled, and Matthew cocked his head toward the bar. "You guys wanna grab something to eat before we split? We've got an early one tomorrow."

"Why the hell not," Mike agreed. He followed Matthew to the bar, Brent grumbling behind them.

"I could eat a horse," Matthew commented as he sat down.

Mike raised his eyebrows. "What the hell did you do all day? I had to haul Christopher's furniture around."

Matthew chuckled. "Let's just say I didn't get much sleep last night. And that rounds two and three took place this morning."

Brent slid onto a stool beside them, his eyes gleaming. "That hottie that I took home from the bonfire was a wild one in bed. I was almost tempted to get her number, ask her to come over again tonight."

"So why didn't you?" Mike asked.

"Not my MO, man. One night only."

Mike resisted the urge to groan. Here Kenley seemed to think he was a jerk, but he wasn't exactly going around sleeping with a different woman every night, now was he? Not that any of it seemed to make a damn bit of difference.

"How'd the move go anyway?" Matthew asked, ordering another beer.

Mike gave a brief update, leaving out the part of coming to the aid of Lexi and Kenley. He sure the hell didn't need any more ribbing from Matthew or Brent tonight, not when the entire evening had left a sour taste in his mouth. He could've been having a nice dinner with Kenley right now, not breaking up bar brawls and listening to stories of the conquests his friends had made.

He rolled his shoulders, relieving some of the tension, and ordered some food. As soon as he ate, he was outta here.

Chapter 9

Kenley sighed as she shut her laptop the next evening. She'd had back-to-back interviews all day long, without even so much as a lunch break. The only upside was the sooner she finished filling the slots for the new contract they'd won in Norfolk, the sooner she could head home. So was that a good thing or not? At the moment, her spa day yesterday with Lexi felt like a million years ago.

She pulled out her phone, texting her best friend:

Crazy day but wanted to check in. How are you feeling today?

Lexi's reply came back instantly:

Feeling much better. Christopher's taking me out for a quiet dinner tonight.

Must be nice, Kenley thought. Then again, Mike had offered to take her out last night. Too bad he was such a pain in her ass. She texted a quick reply back to Lexi:

Sounds perfect. Have fun!

Kenley stood, gathering her belongings. After sitting all day long without a break, she wanted nothing more than a long hot bubble bath and some carry-out for dinner. And maybe a few glasses of wine. She was trying to decide between pizza or Chinese when her cell phone rang. It was the number of her office back in Arlington, so she answered before heading out for the night.

"How'd everything go today?" the head of HR asked.

"Great. I think we can make offers to several of the candidates. I'll email the ones I've selected to you for final approval, and I can get the offer packets ready tomorrow if they accept."

"Wonderful. I'm hoping we can expedite this. We need people starting on this contract immediately. Can you schedule a second interview this week for the candidates we select and then provide the offer letter and new hire materials to them then?"

"Um, maybe," Kenley said, glancing at her stack of papers. That meant twice as much work for her. Normally the home office mailed out the HR materials for new hires. She'd brought a few packets down but didn't have enough for everyone they'd be bringing onboard. And doing an additional round of interviews meant she'd be here twice as long.

"Do you have enough of the materials?"

"For a couple of the candidates, yes, but I don't have enough for everyone. I don't usually need them."

"Of course. We can Fed-Ex them down. I don't suppose I can convince you to drive back up tonight? Pick them up yourself?"

Kenley resisted the urge to groan. The drive to Northern Virginia was four hours from Virginia Beach. She could drive up there, spend the night at her apartment, and then leave early in the morning to get back for her first interview. It wasn't exactly ideal though, especially considering she was already completely exhausted.

"We'll pay you overtime, of course. Travel expenses, as well as compensation for the hours spent driving. You'd be doing me a tremendous favor."

"Yeah, I guess. How late will you be in the office?"

"I've got tons to do, so I'll be here until at least nine. I'll stay and wait for you though."

"Uh, okay. I'll leave here in a little while and drive up."

"Wonderful. Thanks so much, Kenley. I really appreciate your willingness to go the extra mile."

Kenley rolled her eyes. A couple hundred miles was more like it. One extra mile would've been nothing. She said goodbye and tucked her phone into her bag. She wouldn't mind picking up some more work outfits from her apartment at home. And if she had to be back on the road bright and early tomorrow, well, that's what Starbucks was for, right?

***

Mike groaned as he stepped onto the dock back on base, dripping wet. They'd conducted several hours of water drills, getting in dives and rescue simulations. Two boats now bobbed up and down in the ocean as drops of rain began to fall. The sky had darkened from an impending storm, the waters turning choppy during their last hour of training. As tired as he was, for once he was glad they wouldn't have to deal with training in the middle of a storm. Normally he relished the challenge, but after several nights of not sleeping well, he felt like he was running on fumes.

He rolled his shoulders, easing the tension and ache in his muscles. Fucking hell. It wasn't the day on base that had him stiff and sore, it was those damn sleepless nights. He'd spent his twenties up all night and training all day, but hell if the years weren't catching up with him. He was getting too old for this.

"That was fucking spectacular," Brent said, grinning as he peeled down the top of his wetsuit.

"Which part?" Mike asked dryly.

The entire afternoon had blurred into one long session as they dove again and again, practicing various water rescues. The idea had been to leave them drained and fatigued, preparing them for the unknowns they could face when out on an op. Mission accomplished.

"Are you kidding me?" Brent asked. "With the incoming storm, some of those swells were killer."

"Literally," Christopher said, dropping his gear on the ground.

Brent chuffed out a laugh. "Hell, there's nothing better than that."

"I've got to call Lexi when we get inside and let her know I'm running late," Christopher said.

"Big plans?" Mike asked, raising his eyebrows.

"I'm taking her out for a romantic dinner. She needs it after her day yesterday."

"Great idea, man," Evan said as he walked by, slapping Christopher on the back. "I should take Ali out, too."

Jesus, Mike thought. Those guys were totally

whipped. They'd each just spent the weekend with their respective girlfriends. Hell, they *lived* with them. And the second they were back on dry land, they were ready to rush home to woo their women.

"Great job today, men," Patrick said, climbing off of the boat as he addressed the team. "Everyone executed their maneuvers perfectly, with time to spare. Even with this storm rolling in and rougher waters, our times were good in each simulation. Job well done."

The other man grunted in affirmation, with Christopher saying, "Thanks, Ice."

Matthew walked up beside Mike as the men headed in to change. "Remember in the old days when we'd all go to Anchors after a day like today? Now half the team is heading home to their women," he chuckled.

"Don't I know it," Mike agreed.

"I've got half a mind to call one of those pretty nurses from the bonfire," Matthew said, grinning. "You want in? I could get her to bring a friend along. We could take them to dinner and then go our separate ways."

"Nah, not tonight," Mike said. A date with one of those women was literally the last thing he wanted at the moment.

"I heard that," Brent called out. "You still fantasizing about Kenley?"

"I'm not anything with Kenley," Mike ground out, clenching his teeth.

"She was pretty hot; I'd do her," Brent taunted, a gleam in his eye.

"Fucking hell, asshole," Mike spat out over his shoulder. "She's off limits."

"Don't care, huh?" Brent smirked.

Mike muttered under his breath as they walked into base. That guy needed to learn to watch his mouth. He'd laid it on every man on the team at one point or another, and sometimes that shit got old. Some days he and his teammates fought like brothers, but with Brent always running his mouth, he was going to get his ass whipped at some point.

Patrick caught up with them as they walked inside, heading for the locker room. "Did everything go okay last night?"

"With what?" Matthew asked.

"Everything's fine," Mike ground out. Yeah. If a woman leaving you standing by yourself on the sidewalk and shouting at you to leave her alone was anyone's definition of "fine."

"Mike drove Kenley home. Those two are so hot and cold I'm waiting for one of them to spontaneously combust."

"Keep waiting," Mike muttered.

"You had a date, huh? She's a sweet little thing," Matthew drawled.

Mike chuffed out a laugh. "Definitely not a date," he said. "She was with Lexi, and I ended up giving her a lift back to her car. End of story."

"Uh-huh," Matthew grinned. "And I've given up playing the field."

Patrick laughed. "From what I can tell, Mike's all but smitten with Kenley. They might as well send out the wedding invitations now. And that means you could be next," he added pointedly.

"Not a chance in hell," Matthew laughed.

Yeah, Mike thought, because three men on their SEAL team tied down in relationships wasn't enough.

He had no intention of becoming the fourth.

Mike showered and changed in the locker room, pulling his civilian clothes back on. He couldn't decide if he needed caffeine or some shut-eye more. This day was wearing on him. He slammed his locker shut, ready to call it a night. Matthew was on his cell phone making plans with one of the nurses, but Mike waved as he headed out the door.

Fat raindrops had begun to fall from the sky as he jogged across the parking lot on base. He waved to Patrick, who was already pulling out to head home. Ducking into his SUV, Mike started the engine. It was almost seven, which meant he'd been on base for almost twelve hours. Hell of a way to start the week. He tossed his gym bag onto the passenger seat and maneuvered out of the lot, heading home.

Twenty minutes later he was pulling into his driveway. He'd rented a small townhouse near the quieter side of town last year and had enjoyed every second of the peace and quiet—not to mention the extra space. Funnily enough, it wasn't too damn far from that condo Kenley had been staying in. Her parents' condo. Not that he'd tell her that. She'd probably check into a hotel on the beach if she knew he was so close by.

Grabbing his gear, he ran to the front door, sheets of rain coming down from the sky. His shirt was soaked by the time he reached the safety of the front porch. He pulled his cell phone and house keys from his pocket, ready to head in, and was surprised to see three missed calls on the screen from Kenley.

Not even bothering to unlock the door, he stayed on the porch as he dialed his voicemail, sensing something was wrong. Even if she'd had a sudden change of heart and wanted to see him, there's no way she'd call three times in the span of an hour unless there was an emergency.

His heartbeat accelerated as he wondered if something had happened to her. Her panicked voice finally came over the line, and his gut clenched as he heard her crying. The message was muffled, and he cursed as the call disconnected.

The second message started a few seconds later.

"Mike, my car ran off the road in this rainstorm. I don't even know where I am, but I need help. I, I'm sorry about last night, but please call me."

Mike's eyes narrowed. Fucking hell. She thought he wouldn't help her because of the way things had ended between them last night? What kind of jackass did she think he was?

Mike shoved his keys into the lock, pushing open his front door. He dropped his gear down, a resounding *thud* filling the foyer, as he called Kenley's number. It rang and rang, but there was no answer. Scanning the room as if that would somehow give him the answers, he swiped his hand across his brow.

Lexi. Lexi would know where she was. He'd call Christopher, figure out what was going on, and then go find Kenley. The idea of her scared and alone out in this storm was unnerving. Was she injured? Frightened? Stranded but shaken up? Even if she wasn't hurt, being stuck on the side of the road alone at night had to be unsettling. She had to be really upset if she'd call him for help.

Mike cursed and then dialed his friend.

Chapter 10

Kenley twisted in the front seat of her wrecked car, wincing at the pain shooting through her wrist. She was shivering, either from cold or shock. Or maybe both. If she could just open the damn door, she could get out and…what? The rain was pouring down. It was pitch black outside. Her car had run off the highway and into the trees and bushes where no one could find her. What did she think simply getting out of her vehicle would accomplish? Then she'd be soaking wet, stranded, and in pain.

Reaching over, she fumbled around her glove compartment until she found a flashlight. She tried turning it on with her good arm, but to no avail. Dead.

"Damn it!" she shouted, tossing it onto the passenger seat as tears streamed down her face.

She slumped back into her seat, trying to take deep breaths and calm down. Easier said than done after a tractor trailer cut you off, sending you swerving off the damn road. Her car had spun out on the wet pavement, and the next thing she knew, she was crashing into bushes and trees. Stuck. Stranded.

She blew out a breath in exasperation. If worst came to worst, they'd find her in the morning. Certainly her car had left tire marks or indentations on the grass as she'd veered off the highway. Maybe she could wrap something around her wrist to ease some of the pain. And she had to have some pain killers in her purse. That might tide her over until help arrived.

She tried dialing 911 again, but the signal kept dropping. The rain and the damn forest weren't exactly helping her get a strong signal. If she could just get out of her car, maybe she could make it back to highway and flag someone down. Or get a strong enough signal from a cell tower to call for help. She tried the door again, shoving against it as best she could, but it was stuck. She might have hit something as the car veered into the foliage.

Unbuckling her seatbelt, Kenley climbed over the center console and onto the passenger seat. Gingerly, she tried that door.

Bingo. It opened.

The smell of damp forest filled her nostrils. It was woodsy and clean and exactly not what she wanted to be stuck in the middle of.

Rain poured down from the sky, rustling branches and leaves. It fell hard and heavy, filling the forest with nothing but its sound, drowning out the highway that was probably only feet away. She couldn't see a damn thing, but at least she could get out.

She grabbed her cell phone again, noticing how

low the battery was getting. Her heart pounded in anticipation. If the battery died before she could get a hold of someone, then she really would be stuck here all night.

Another tear slid down her cheek as she thought about how she could've been taking a nice hot bubble bath right now. In desperation, she tried Lexi's number. Somehow the call went through, and she left a frantic message. Tears streaming down her cheeks, she saw Mike's number beside Lexi's in her contact list. He was the last person on Earth she wanted to talk to, but he'd help her. He'd know what to do.

***

"I'll run a trace on her number," Christopher said. "If she was using her cell to call you and Lexi, hopefully it's still turned on. But even if it's not, I can see the last cell tower location that it pinged. That should give you a general idea of where she is."

"Thanks, man," Mike said. "I figure she can't be too far. I'll start driving over the bridge. Text me the coordinates."

"Sure thing. And let us know when you find her. Lexi is freaking out."

"So am I," Mike muttered. "I figure she wouldn't call me unless it was a last resort type thing."

"Lexi called the state troopers while I was running the search. They'll be out looking for her, too. We've got an edge though since we're already a few steps ahead of them."

"Shit, man, is tracing her number like that even legal?"

"Don't ask. But I'd do it for anyone who was in

danger. And don't worry—they won't even know I was there."

Mike laughed, feeling a brief moment of levity. "I'm surprised Lexi didn't hack into the cell tower records herself."

"Hell, she would've if she wasn't so stressed out. No worries, I'll have the location for you in a few minutes.

"Good. Thanks, man, I owe you," he said, disconnecting with Christopher.

Apparently Kenley had been headed home in this mess. What the hell had made her want to drive back to Northern Virginia in this freaking monsoon? The storms that blew in off the ocean in this area could be surprisingly strong; the flooding that came from them dangerous and deadly. Had Kenley even checked the forecast before rushing home tonight?

He blew out a breath as he grabbed his keys and made a dash to his SUV. If she'd worked all day in Norfolk before leaving, she was probably still on I-64, the long stretch of highway that connected the Virginia Beach area to Williamsburg and Richmond. Good. That meant he'd get to her sooner. And sooner was about all he could handle at the moment.

His chest tightened at the idea of Kenley out there alone. Why she had him so worked up, he didn't even want to fully examine.

But he cared about her. And just like she'd rushed down to help Lexi when she was in trouble, Mike would do the same for her. He owed her that much. And if anything else came from it, well, they'd just cross that bridge when they came to it.

Chapter 11

Kenley sank back into the passenger seat. She'd tried making her way to the road, but it was nearly impossible in the darkness and rain. She'd stumbled once, nearly twisting her ankle, and she didn't need that on top of her injured wrist. If no one found her soon, she'd just have to wait until morning. She didn't have a working flashlight, she only had use of one hand—at the rate she was going, she'd probably fall and break her leg in the dark.

She peeled off her wet coat, shivering. At least she had plenty of gas in her tank, so she could start the engine and crank up the heat. And when the rain stopped, she could try honking the horn and setting off the car alarm in hopes of getting attention of a passing vehicle. No one would hear her in this downpour though.

She climbed back into the driver's seat, wincing in pain when she moved her left hand. She had to have something in the car she could wrap her wrist in.

A loud crack of thunder boomed across the sky, and she jumped. It was ridiculous that she'd run just off the road—she felt so close yet so far away. There were probably hundreds of cars driving by at the moment, and not a single one knew she was here.

She hoped and prayed that Lexi and Mike had gotten her messages and called 911. All of her other friends and family were still in Northern Virginia. No, scratch that—her parents were off on another luxury European cruise. They rarely stuck around for long, preferring instead to spend their retirement traveling. They'd also spent her childhood doing the same, but hey, who was keeping score.

She closed her eyes as she let the heat warm her. After the day she was having, she probably could fall asleep sitting up right here. Normally that sounded downright uncomfortable, but she was exhausted. Maybe if she just rested for a few minutes she'd feel better....

"Kenley!" a deep voice shouted. Someone pounded on the window. "Kenley!"

She bolted up in shock and screamed. A bright flashlight beamed in the window at her, and she shrunk back into her seat in fear. She felt like an animal on display on the zoo—there was nowhere to hide, nowhere to seek shelter. What if some ax murderer or rapist had found her? She'd been startled from a deep sleep and suddenly a man was banging on the glass and shouting.... But wait—wasn't he calling her name?

"Damn it, Kenley, answer me!" a gruff voice shouted. "Are you okay?"

"I can't open the door!" she yelled back.

The man banged on it again, yanking on the door handle, but didn't have any more luck than she did in her attempts earlier.

"Hang on, I'll get you out!"

"The other side," she said, uselessly pointing. It was doubtful he could see her movements in the darkened interior, even with that bright light. She crawled over to the passenger seat again, tears streaming down her cheeks as she accidentally put pressure on her wrist. The flashlight and its owner rounded the front of her car, and a second later, the passenger door was opening.

The car's interior light popped on, and her heart pounded frantically she looked up into the worried face of Mike. He'd come for her? Even after she'd blown him off last night? Yes, she'd called both Lexi and him in panic earlier, but she'd expected they'd call the police or something. The last person on Earth she expected to see coming to her rescue was the man she'd told to leave her alone.

Relief flooded through her as Mike ducked down, no doubt getting soaked as he crouched on the wet ground beside her vehicle. At least all that damn rain had finally stopped.

"Kenley, honey…."

"Mike," she sobbed, the tears flowing freely as she began to tremble. She'd never been so happy to see someone in her entire life.

"Come here," he soothed, pulling her toward him.

She fell into his embrace, letting her head rest on his solid chest. He had on a jacket over his clothes, but she felt warm and safe just having him hold her. One hand slid to the back of her head, holding her to him, like she was something precious he wanted to cherish and care for.

"Kenley, sweetheart, are you okay?" She felt his deep timbre reverberate in her chest, warming her to the very soul. His scent surrounded her, and she relaxed into him, knowing she'd be okay.

"It hurts," she whimpered.

"What does, angel?"

"My wrist."

Mike reached out and gently held her wrist with one large hand, running his fingers over her delicate bones. She winced in pain, and he clenched his jaw. "Let me put a splint on this; it may be broken. I'll get you out of here and take you to the hospital for x-rays. We'll call the state troopers when we're back in my SUV. They're all out looking for you, but I can't get any good reception here."

"Thanks for coming to find me," she whispered.

"It wasn't even a question," Mike assured her.

She nodded, and he pulled her back into his arms, kissing the top of her head. "Lexi was really worried about you," he said. "So was I after I got your message."

"How'd you find me?"

Mike gently pulled back, his hands resting on her shoulders. She met his concerned blue gaze.

"Christopher and Lexi. They hacked into the phone network and pinged the last location of your cell phone. Not sure how legal that is, but they weren't going to wait around until the police could locate you."

"A tractor trailer changed lanes, and I swerved. My car started to spin on the wet pavement, and the next thing I knew, I was crashing into the trees. I tried to hike back up the embankment to the highway once I finally got out of the car, but I couldn't in the rain with my injured wrist. I'm not even sure if the other driver knew he ran me off the road."

"What a jackass. We'll have to teach you some defensive driving maneuvers."

"I don't know if that would've helped."

"Honey, when I'm done with you, you'll be able to handle anything."

Kenley let out a small laugh. "Can we go now?"

"Absolutely. Let me wrap your wrist, and we'll be on our way."

***

Two hours later, Mike helped Kenley back into his SUV. She clutched her injured arm to her stomach, and he helped her fasten the seatbelt. After a quick trip to the ER, she now had a small cast on her wrist. She looked completely exhausted, and Mike wanted nothing more than to take her back to his townhouse, where he could take care of her, keep an eye on her— and keep her safely tucked away in his own bed all night long.

"Where were you headed tonight anyway?" he asked as he pulled onto the highway leading back toward Virginia Beach.

"My boss wanted me to pick up some paperwork at home."

"And they couldn't just fax it to you?" Mike asked in disbelief.

"She said they could Fed Ex it down, but I needed a ton of new hire packages right away—company brochures, health care benefits, that sort of thing. The contract we won is big, and we're bringing on a large number of people. That's why I stayed down here—to help with the hiring process. We have a need for immediate hires, so my boss was hoping to expedite things."

"So your boss thought you could just drive home late at night to retrieve them. Why didn't he just bring them down here himself if he was so damn concerned?"

"She. And I don't know. If I'd thought of it, maybe I would've suggested that myself. It would've saved me the trouble—and that God-awful accident. Now I have a fractured wrist, a damaged car.... Shit, is my car still there?"

"Already taken care of," Mike reassured her.

"It is?"

"Yeah, when you were getting x-rays, I spoke with the state troopers, and we had it towed out. There was minimal damage, which is good news. You went straight off the road and avoided hitting anything big. Matthew and Christopher went to pick it up."

"But why would they do that? It's totally out of their way."

Mike shrugged. "It needed to be done. You can't be driving long distances with your injured wrist. I guess your boss will have to find another way to get all of that paperwork to you."

"Shit," Kenley muttered. "I didn't even call her." She rummaged around in her purse, looking for her cell phone. "And my phone died. Ugh!"

"You can use mine," Mike said, pulling it from his pocket.

"Thanks."

Mike listened in as Kenley dialed her home office and explained the situation to her boss. Kenley sighed as she disconnected the call. "She said she'd find another way to get them down to Virginia Beach and told me just to rest up."

"Well at least she has some common sense," Mike muttered. The fact that the woman had expected Kenley to rush the four hours home after a long day at work didn't sit well with him. Was she expecting Kenley to drive back down here in the middle of the night, too? Then go in to work tomorrow on no sleep? It shouldn't be his concern to worry about her, but hell. He'd been terrified himself when he got her message. A crying and frightened Kenley was not something he wanted to hear—ever.

She stifled a yawn beside him, and he glanced her way. "Why don't you rest? You've had a long night, and it'll still be another hour before we're back."

"Um, okay," she said, her eyelids slipping shut. "Maybe just for a minute."

"Kenley?" he asked softly a minute later.

She was already sound asleep.

Mike resisted the urge to grin. Although he didn't like the idea of Kenley being injured, he'd seen a completely different side of her tonight. She hadn't fought him, hadn't told him off. She'd actually *needed* him. She'd let him help her, let him hold her. And hell if that didn't make him feel like the greatest guy in the world. He was used to helping others, protecting the defenseless, coming to the aid of people in need. But when the woman he was secretly falling for looked at him that way? When she fell into his arms like she belonged there? Pure magic.

Chapter 12

Kenley abruptly woke up when a car door slammed shut. Groggily, she remembered Mike had driven her home from the ER. In the streetlight, she watched Mike as he rounded the front of the SUV to come over and assist her, looking as calm and steady as he had all evening. He'd tucked his coat around her after she'd fallen asleep, and he looked muscular and fit in a thermal knit Henley top and another pair of khaki cargo pants. No matter what, Mike always looked like he was ready to roll into action. He could probably sling some gear over his shoulder and take off on a mission, simple as that.

But where were they right now? Even in her half-awake state, she could see she wasn't at her parents' condo. Her parents. She should probably call them, let them know about the accident. Assure them that she was okay. But how would she even reach them on a cruise ship? She didn't even know their itinerary or port of call.

She sighed. Once again, they weren't around. Of course she was a grown woman now, fully capable of taking care of herself. But that didn't mean she wouldn't mind having them in the same country as her every once in a while. Was that too much to ask?

Mike quietly opened the passenger door. "Wake up, sleeping beauty," he gently teased.

"I'm already awake," she said, but a smile spread across her face. "Where are we? Didn't we make it back?"

"My place," Mike said, reaching in to help her get out of the SUV.

"Your place? You can drop me off at my condo. I'm fine."

"Not a chance."

Kenley raised her eyebrows.

"Hell, sweetheart, if you really don't want to stay here, I'll take you over to Lexi's and Christopher's. But you shouldn't be alone."

"Mike, they checked me out at the hospital. I'm fine."

Mike looked pointedly at her wrist.

"Okay, so not *fine* fine. But taken care of. My wrist is in a cast. It'll heal."

"And I'll feel better knowing I can keep an eye on you tonight."

"Look, that's nice of you, but all I want to do is take a long hot shower. And eat something."

"Done and done. And hey, there's even a huge bathtub you can use if you want."

Kenley sighed. She was too tired to argue, and a bath sounded pretty spectacular right now. But spending the night at Mike's house? Even if it was under the premise of him watching over her, that didn't seem like an option she should entertain at the moment. She had too many unsettled feelings about him. Physically she was attracted to him, but the fact that he'd rushed to find her warmed her up in an entirely different way. It was sweet and protective. Not sides of Mike that she usually saw.

He slipped an arm around her waist, pulling her to him. She felt safe tucked against his large frame. He handed her the purse she'd left in his SUV and then shut the door, guiding her up the steps to his townhouse. "I've never brought a woman here before," he admitted.

Kenley had to remember how to keep her legs moving.

That was…unexpected. "Never?"

"Nope. Just rented it a year ago. I was getting tired of living with roommates all the damn time. Sometimes a man needs his own space."

"But you want to bring me here?"

Mike met her gaze. "There's nothing I want more." Heat flashed in his eyes, quickly replaced by something else. Tenderness, perhaps. He'd been worried about her. That much was obvious with the way he'd rushed to find her and stayed with her in the ER all night. Not that Mike or any of the guys would've left her alone and stranded in a hospital, but her heart melted a little bit at all the concern he'd shown.

She nodded as Mike opened the front door, not ready to share her own thoughts. It was surreal enough even being here with him. Every other time they'd been together they'd argued. And tonight? The thought hadn't even crossed her mind.

They stepped inside, and Kenley unwittingly scanned the room. His place was sparsely furnished, but clean. Neat. For a man used to the regimented life of a Navy SEAL, she supposed it made sense. Suited him, even. He probably wasn't even around that much. She'd only known him for a few weeks, so she couldn't say for sure. But Mike and the rest of the guys probably deployed all the time. Which was exactly why she'd never end up with a man like him.

"The bath's in the master bathroom," Mike said, nodding to the stairs. "I'll get you some towels and stuff—maybe a change of clothes?"

"Uh, yeah. Okay."

"Ladies first," Mike said, nodding to the stairs. She didn't relish the idea of Mike walking behind her, staring at her ass the entire way up, but what was she supposed to do?

She started up the stairs, feeling intrusive as she looked around Mike's home. But why should that bother her? He'd all but barged into her parents' condo and grabbed her. Certainly she had a right to look around a place he'd invited her to.

A few framed awards hung on the walls leading up the stairs—mostly military stuff she didn't even know the meaning of. Obviously he was proud of his work as a SEAL—as he should be. Mike and all those guys worked hard to get where they were today. She didn't know the entire process to become a SEAL, but she knew it was grueling. More men failed than made it all the way.

Mike placed a hand on the small of her back, guiding her into his bedroom. She stilled, suddenly feeling hesitant. "It's okay," Mike said, his voice deep. "The bathroom's right over here."

She walked across the room, Mike never leaving her side. "Let me grab you some clean towels," he said as they walked into the spacious master bath.

There was a large soaking tub next to a shower stall, and Mike's razor and toothbrush sat lined up neatly on the counter top. He turned on the bathtub for her after grabbing some towels, and steam began to fill the room.

"So do you soak in the tub much?" Kenley asked with a smirk.

Mike glanced back at her and winked. "Not even once." His gaze slid to the cast on her wrist. "Is that waterproof?"

"No. I'll have to just rest it on the side of the tub."

"Do you need any help?" he asked, his eyes gentling.

"I think I'm okay," she said, suddenly feeling shy. She was attracted to Mike, yes, but not once had she imagined them bathing together. Especially after running off the road and spending an evening in the ER. And all those times she'd imagined his body moving over hers, commanding her into a pleasured frenzy, she'd been relaxed and content, not frazzled and wearing an ugly cast.

She glanced down at the button-down shirt she'd worn to work today. They'd rolled up the sleeve to put the cast on her wrist, but would she even be able to slip her arm out over the bulkiness? It would also be difficult fumbling around with the buttons with only one hand, but what was she supposed to do? It's not like she was going to ask Mike to undress her. She glanced up to find him watching her, and her cheeks flamed.

"Let me help you," he said, stepping closer. She

looked up to meet his gaze, and he gently cupped her cheek in one hand. Her heart palpitated in her chest, and she couldn't resist leaning into his touch. "I want to take care of you," he said, his voice gravel.

"Mike…."

"Let me take care of you, Kenley."

She trembled as one hand slid to her waist, but she didn't pull away like she had the other night at the beach. He was so close, she could feel his warmth, smell his scent. He was wordlessly pulling her toward him again, drawing her in until resistance was futile. Nothing would stop her from being with him tonight. She was tired of fighting her feelings, of acting like nothing was there. They were here, together, and she needed him. Wanted him.

His grip tightened ever so slightly, and Mike dipped his head lower, holding her gaze. As she held her breath, his lips finally brushed against hers. His kiss was soft, gentle. Completely at odds with the hardened warrior and aggressive alpha male that was Mike. He was taking it slow with her, sensing her needs tonight, and that was all she could ask for.

Mike deepened the kiss as she gasped, all the desire and tension that had been working its way through her finally about to explode to the surface. Her hands came to his chest, and he gently gripped the fingers of her injured one. "Are you okay?" he asked between kisses.

"Yes," she said breathlessly.

"Damn, the bath," he said, rushing over to turn it off before it reached overflow proportions. "Guess I got a little distracted," he said with a crooked grin.

"Just a little," she agreed.

"You're the best kind of distraction," he said

quietly as his eyes bore into hers. They were wide with arousal, and she wasn't imagining the bulge forming in his pants. He wanted her.

"Is that so?" she teased, suddenly feeling more confident.

"Uh huh," he said, taking a step toward her. "I could let you distract me all night."

Mike prowled back over until he towered above her, and she tilted her head back to meet his searing gaze. His hands found the top button of her blouse, gently undoing it as she tried to remember how to breathe. His eyes heated, and he moved lower and lower, his knuckles occasionally brushing against her bare skin, driving her absolutely out of her mind. What she wouldn't give to feel them dragging all over her body.

A moment later, her blouse fell completely open, revealing her to him. Delicate lace covered her breasts, and she was relieved she'd at least put something nice on today. She certainly wasn't expecting for Mike to undress her tonight. That had literally been the very last way she'd expected to end her day.

"You're so gorgeous, Kenley," he said. "Even more beautiful now than at the pool."

His fingertips gently traced over her collarbone, sending shivers down her spine. He ducked down, kissing her along the same path his fingers had taken. His lips and hot breath on her skin was almost more than she could bear. Her chest heaved with every breath she took, and Mike let out a low rumble of approval.

"You smell so sweet. Like vanilla," he murmured. The scruff of his five o'clock shadow rubbed against her sensitive skin, driving her crazy. She wanted his kisses, his touch, everywhere. She needed to feel him rasping against her skin, kissing her, claiming her as his own.

Mike slid her blouse over her bare shoulders, his fingers lightly brushing against her skin, and down her arms, the sleeve catching on her cast.

"I don't think it's going to come off," she said.

"I might have to cut it."

She nodded; then he left the bathroom and came back a moment later. After gently removing her shirt, Mike pulled his own up over his head. His bare chest and torso were amazing, all rippling muscles and tanned, smooth skin. She'd seen him at the pool but hadn't wanted to gawk or let him know that she was paying any attention. But right now? She wanted to run her hands all over that hot, male flesh, laving attention on him, doing a little exploring of her own.

"I want to see all of you," he said huskily, stepping closer. Kenley backed against the door, and suddenly Mike was there, kissing her, pressing his hard body against hers. Her hands trailed over his abdomen, running across his broad pecs. She could feel his thick erection rubbing against her belly, and her panties dampened. She ached for him—needed him inside her, filling her completely, making her whole.

Mike's hands slid behind her back, undoing the clasp of her bra, and he carefully slid it down her arms, over her cast. Cool air washed over her breasts, startling even in the steamy bathroom. Her nipples beaded, and Mike ducked his head down, kissing her around one areola and then sucking a nipple into his greedy mouth. His tongue flicked back and forth over the sensitive bud, and she cried out, the sensation shooting straight to her core.

She gasped as he palmed her other breast, kneading and caressing her. His large hands on her skin was driving her absolutely crazy. She felt small and feminine next to him, delicate compared to his broad shoulders and wall of muscles. But the way he was so attentive to her? It would practically be her undoing.

"Mike," she gasped as his knuckles skimmed across her bare stomach.

He unbuttoned her pants with one hand, easing the zipper down, and reached in, palming her sex. The way his large hand cupped her was sexy and intimate, not to mention possessive as hell. His lips found her mouth again, and this time his tongue sought entrance, sweeping inside as he claimed her. His knuckles ran lightly over her clit, and even through her lace panties, she arched back and gasped at his intimate caress. "Does that feel good, baby?" he asked huskily, tugging her earlobe between his teeth.

"Yes," she pleaded.

He chuckled and pulled her pants down, slowly peeling her panties down afterward. "Are you wet for me?" he asked.

"Yes," she whimpered as his fingers slid through her soft folds, teasing and exploring.

"Fuck, Kenley," he moaned. "Later on I want to taste all that sweet flesh."

He quickly shucked his own pants and boxer briefs, and she watched his erection spring out. He was thick and hard and so very ready. A bead of pre-cum appeared on the swollen head, and she felt a surge of wonder knowing he was that aroused because of her.

"Tell me you're on the pill."

"Yes."

"I'm clean, I promise. Let me take you like this. Completely bare?"

She had a feeling it was the only question he'd be asking tonight. Mike was otherwise in complete and utter control.

"Yes," she whispered.

"Thank God," he muttered. Mike bent and picked her up, his muscled arms easily lifting her, and carried her to the bath. "Keep your arm above the water," he instructed.

He settled down into the large tub, holding her securely against him. Warm water surrounded them, and it was sexy as hell having Mike hold her to him this way as the water lapped against them. His erection ground into her bottom, and she resisted the urge to wiggle against him.

Leaning back, he guided her head to rest on his shoulder. A towel on the side of the tub cushioned her injured arm, and water lapped around her breasts, barely peeking out above the water.

Mike held her for a moment, letting the water and steam surround them. It felt good to be in his muscular arms, his powerful body holding her safe and secure. At the moment she couldn't imagine ever wanting to be anywhere else.

He lowered his head and kissed her slowly, his lips gently caressing hers. He tasted of mint and man, sinfully good. His tongue lightly traced the seam of her lips, and she opened to him, letting him have control of the kiss. Large hands palmed her breasts as arousal pooled at her center, and she was suddenly aching, desperate for him to touch her intimately. He pulled and plucked at her nipples, teasing her, until finally she was writhing in his lap. One hand slid down between her breasts, over the soft curve of her stomach, and lower still until her finally reached her center. Mike's thick fingers slid through her folds, touching, caressing, teasing.

"Spread your legs for me." She did as he asked, and he hooked one of her legs over his own, opening her even wider to him.

"God, Kenley, I love seeing you like this."

He spread her arousal around, and she gasped as he penetrated her with one thick finger, slowly working it in and out until he added a second. He slowly filled and stretched her, readying her for him, and her walls clamped down around him as she moaned in pleasure.

"You're so tight, baby. And I'm going to make you feel so good."

He circled her clit, spreading her arousal over her throbbing bud. Heat coiled down from her center as she gasped. Waves of pleasure began to build as he moved faster and faster, and Kenley bucked helplessly against him, finally crying out, arching back further into his arms. Mike continued to stroke her gently until she finally fell back down from heaven, limp and sated.

He lifted her and easily turned her around, readjusting the towel for her to rest her arm. She settled back into his lap, her legs spread on either side of his hips, and she felt his throbbing cock rubbing against her slickened sex. Mike gripped her waist, lifting her, and then he thrust upward as he pulled her back down, impaling her completely.

She gasped at the intimate invasion, moaning in

pleasure at the exquisite pressure of him buried deep inside her. She felt so full, so good, the moment almost danced between pleasure and pain. He stilled for a moment, allowing her to get used to him, then slowly began to move in and out, stroking her inner walls. Mike ducked down and kissed her again, and she cried out in pleasure as the base of his penis rubbed against her still swollen clit. He thrust again and again, faster and faster, and she gasped, seeing stars.

Mike gripped her hips tightly and held her to him as he claimed her, stealing her breath, capturing her soul, sending her soaring once more.

Chapter 13

Mike groaned in pleasure as Kenley's inner walls tightened once more around him. The way she'd straddled him in the bathtub was sexy as fuck, her full breasts bouncing up and down, her cascading brown curls falling around her shoulders. She looked like some sort of goddess right out of a painting. Watching her come as he'd thrust into her over and over was pure heaven. He'd just driven her to ecstasy with his fingers moments before, and she was already coming again on his throbbing cock. She clamped down around him like a vice, her slickened sex feeling like damn near perfection.

He held onto her waist, driving himself into her harder and faster. As her breasts bounced up and down and she threw her head back, he shattered, spilling his seed deep inside her molten core.

He muttered an oath as he came harder than he ever had before. He'd always used condoms in the past, never daring to go without. But hell, with Kenley he wanted it all. He'd have her come on his tongue before the night was over. He'd have to be careful with her injured wrist, but there was nothing he wanted more than to enjoy her in as many ways as possible. To tease her and pleasure her until she was begging for mercy. Until she admitted she was his and his alone.

"Fuck, baby, you feel so good," he said as he slowly fell back down to Earth. He pulled Kenley to his chest, holding her close even as he was still buried balls deep inside of her. She was panting and breathless, and her lips brushing against his neck felt like the kiss of an angel. He wanted to scoop her up, keep her safe, and never let her go.

"That was…wow," she murmured.

Mike chuckled quietly. He planned to show her exactly how many ways he could "wow" her tonight. He gently eased Kenley up and pulled out, turning her and setting her back down on his lap.

"Let me wash your hair," he murmured. Hell, he'd never offered to wash a woman's hair before in his life. But even if she wasn't in a cast, he had a feeling he'd want to do it for Kenley. She stirred up feelings of protectiveness inside him that he'd never had for a woman before.

He turned the bath back on, running more hot water, and poured some of it over Kenley's head. After he grabbed a bottle of his shampoo, he began massaging it into Kenley's hair. She closed her eyes and actually *moaned*. Hell, one of these days he'd stretch her out on his bed and give her a full body massage that would have her moaning like she wouldn't believe. And that massage would be guaranteed to have a *very* happy ending.

He rinsed her hair, the suds from the shampoo washing down across her bare shoulders, breasts, and back. She wouldn't smell like vanilla anymore, she'd smell like *him*. His cock rose to attention at that thought. Kenley was his.

She giggled and gently rubbed her ass against him. "Ready again, sailor?"

"With you, I'm always ready. Let's get cleaned up and then I'm taking you to bed."

Mike washed her gently, paying careful attention to her voluptuous breasts. Hell, he could spend all night just kissing and suckling them. Could she come just from his playing with her nipples? She'd seemed sensitive before, and he was dying to find out.

Quickly scrubbing himself off, he helped her to stand. The water began gurgling as it swirled down the drain, and he assisted Kenley in stepping out of the tub before drying them each off with some fluffy towels.

"Is your arm okay?"

"A little sore; I think the painkillers might be wearing off."

"I'll get you some aspirin."

Mike captured her from behind in a bear hug, loving the feel of her smaller body in his arms. He ducked his head to her ear, nibbling on it before asking if she wanted dinner or bed. Her stomach rumbled before she could answer, and Mike chuckled. "Dinner first then. And I got so distracted by taking a bath with you, I forget to call Christopher and tell them we made it back safely. Do you want to call Lexi while I heat something up?"

"So you cook, too?" Kenley asked, wiggling

around to look up at him. "When you're not out saving the world?"

"For you I will," he said with a wicked grin. "Besides, I need you to keep your energy up. I've got a long night planned."

Kenley blushed as Mike raised his eyebrows. "Honey, we just made love in my bathtub. You don't need to blush around me."

"Stop, you're embarrassing me," she said, lightly swatting him on the chest.

Mike smirked. That was about the cutest thing he'd ever seen. Like she could really stop his teasing. It was cuter than hell the way she blushed around him. And sexy as fuck when she came.

"Hell, I'd eat you for dinner and be satisfied. But instead I'll just have to save that sweet little pussy of yours for dessert."

He turned and strode toward the door, glancing back over her shoulder to wink. Kenley was standing there, mouth agape, clutching the bath towel. And she was about to dress in his clothes. There was something damn satisfying about having her here. About bathing her, cooking for her, and having her in his home. And after dinner, he planned to have her in as many ways as possible.

***

"Are you okay, baby?" Mike asked as he grinned up at her. Kenley had screamed louder than she ever had in her life as Mike made her come on his tongue. She was surprised the neighbors weren't currently dialing 911. Holy hell. What that man could do with his mouth was absolutely sinful.

"Okay?" she asked breathlessly. "After that, I don't think I'll ever be okay again. That was amazing."

Mike chuckled. "That's how I plan to wake you up in the morning. Fair warning," he said with a wink.

Jesus. She didn't think she could survive another one of his Earth-shattering orgasms.

Mike prowled back up her body, kissing her softly on the stomach, slowly kissing the underside of one breast before sucking one nipple into his mouth. She writhed and moaned beneath him, still sensitive and sore from all the attention he'd laved on her all evening. Every pull of her nipple she felt in her still throbbing clit, and at the moment, she wouldn't be surprised if she orgasmed again. Mike was that good.

He had cooked dinner for them, a simple pasta and chicken dish that had been delicious. She'd spoken briefly to Lexi while he'd whipped everything up in the kitchen, and the meal had surprisingly been relaxed and comfortable. She thought she'd be embarrassed after making love in the bath with him, but he'd been attentive and sweet. He'd even offered to pick up some clothes at her condo for her if that would make her feel more comfortable, but she'd decided everything else could wait until morning.

Matthew had briefly swung by, dropping off her car and keys, and she'd flushed as his gaze had swept over her in Mike's clothing. He'd winked before he left, and it had embarrassed her to the core having his friends knowing she was here. She knew Christopher had been waiting in the car, and what Matthew told him would of course make it back to Lexi. Her best friend would be dying for details tomorrow, but for the night, she planned to just enjoy being here with

Mike.

They'd enjoy each other, maybe even see each other again this week or next. But before long, she'd be leaving. She'd be back at home in Arlington. Flings weren't exactly her thing, and she certainly would never get into a serious relationship with a Navy SEAL who was gone half that time. But for the moment? She was done fighting the sizzling chemistry between them.

And right now in his bedroom? Holy hell. He was attentive in a whole other kind of way. Kenley didn't even want to imagine all the women he'd been with to become such an expert on the female form. He seemed to make her rise higher and higher each time he touched her. Make her climax that much harder. Was it like that with everyone? She'd never flown so high in her life as with Mike. The chemistry between them was off-the-charts amazing. Part of her wanted to run the other way, protecting herself from the inevitable hurt that had to follow a night as great as this. And another part of her wanted to never leave, to submit to his control over her body in the bedroom.

Those full male lips that had been expertly kissing all her bare flesh finally reached her mouth. He claimed her, kissing her aggressively, sweeping his tongue inside to explore and conquer. He tasted slightly of beer and spice. And it was good. So, so good.

"How's your arm feeling?" he asked huskily.

"I'm okay, Mike," she replied, wrapping her arms around his neck. His broad shoulders were heavenly, and although she felt slightly awkward holding him this way with her cast, she wanted him closer. His thick erection pushed against her sensitive inner thigh, and she wanted him in her, moving over her, exactly like this. She'd rode him in the bathtub, but she needed to feel his powerful body holding her down on his bed, making her his once more.

"Thank God. Because tonight I plan to make you come so many times, you can't see straight."

"That's quite a promise."

"I've wanted you since the first moment I laid eyes on you," he said, his voice gravel. "Having you here in my bed is like a fantasy come true."

"I wanted you, too," Kenley admitted.

"Since when?" he asked, nipping at her neck. His teeth grazed across her sensitive skin, and she shivered.

"Since the night at the condo. When you held me against the wall, holding my wrists, pressing your body against mine…." She trailed off, embarrassed. She wasn't used to talking about sex this way. Or wanting a man so much. She'd always had safe, predictable sex before. It was nice but nothing spectacular. Nothing even close to the rush she had with Mike. Never had a man demanded anything of her, commanded her to do anything. And now? She loved the way Mike controlled their lovemaking, taking charge without question. It was like he knew exactly what her body craved and gave it to her. Over and over again.

"I was so hard for you then. Just like I am right now," he teased, rubbing his erection up against her slick folds. He was so hot and ready for her, she was desperate to feel him penetrating her again, pushing deep inside her core.

"Mmm, you feel so good…."

"I'm sorry your wrist is fractured, baby. Because I'd love to pin you down right here, driving into you until you come on my cock."

Kenley blushed furiously, her breasts swelling and nipples tightening in arousal. She'd never before wanted a man to treat her that way—to hold her down hard as he took her. But the idea of Mike making her come that way was incredibly arousing.

"Hell, I'd love to tie your wrists up and blindfold you. Make you beg me for mercy."

She gasped, and Mike met her gaze. His fingertips trailed gently across her lips. "What are you thinking?" he asked.

"I, I've never done anything like that before."

"I'd make it so good for you," he assured her. "Of course I wouldn't tie your wrists together now—not with your cast. But I could blindfold you. Would you like that?"

"What…what would you do?"

His eyes heated. "Pleasure you. Make you come harder than you ever have before."

"Um, I don't think…."

"Another time," he whispered, kissing her lightly. "I can make you feel good just like this." He lined the tip of his erection up to her center and edged slightly inside, holding himself there.

"Mike," she pleaded.

He pulled out slightly and then thrust into her again, filling her completely as she gasped. Her sex was so swollen and ready for him, she immediately adjusted to accommodate his large size. When Mike slid inside her, he slaked a need she couldn't even begin to understand. Her body ached for him, for his fullness inside her, for the weight of his body covering her.

His hand slid to where their bodies joined, and he rubbed his thumb over her clit, causing her to cry out. Gently pumping into her sex as he toyed with her had her flying in seconds. She cried out as waves of pleasure washed over her, as she surrendered yet again to his control. This man would be her very undoing, and she had absolutely no power to stop any of it.

Chapter 14

Kenley moaned the next morning, waves of pleasure washing over her as sunlight streamed in the room. She felt relaxed and content in the comfortable bed, and she shut her eyes more tightly, not wanting this delicious dream to end. Heat was spiraling down from her core, setting all of her nerve endings on fire. Her entire body pulsed with pleasure. Reaching down, she felt Mike's head right where she needed him, pleasuring her like he'd done last night. God, she never wanted it to end. What he did with his mouth and his tongue was magic, and if she thought she'd come hard from their lovemaking, it had been nothing compared to Mike going down on her.

She gasped, arching her hips up to meet his clever mouth. He eagerly increased the flicks of his tongue, simply devouring her. Shockwaves of pleasure rocked through her, the exquisite feeling almost too much to bear.

The sensations stopped for just a moment as she opened her eyes, and she gasped in shock at the sight of Mike crouched on the bed, holding her legs apart. "Good morning, baby," he murmured, smug male satisfaction crossing his face.

"Mike...."

He slung her legs up over his broad shoulders, opening her even more to him. He'd told her last night that he planned to wake her up this way this morning, but she'd thought he'd been teasing. This was too much, too good—she was going to explode only seconds after waking.

Mike slid his hands under her bottom, pulling her closer to his face. She squealed with pleasure, and he continued his erotic kiss. She was helpless to this man, her legs splayed over his shoulders, her sex wide open and his for the taking. He held her to him so she couldn't have moved away if she'd wanted to.

And holy hell, she never wanted this pleasure to end.

His tongue lapped at her clit, sending her higher and higher with each stroke. She cried out, nearing the precipice, and he sucked her throbbing bud into his mouth. His ministrations got faster and faster, and she screamed out his name, bucking wildly against his face as she came on his tongue.

Mike didn't let up, drawing every last ounce of pleasure out of her as she writhed and clutched the sheets in her hand. The arm in a cast lay heavy on the bed, and she was spent, exhausted from the Earth-shattering orgasm. He kissed her softly on her nether lips before letting her legs down and shooting her a lazy grin.

"You taste like a fucking goddess, Kenley. I'm

going to wake you up like that every damn morning. I can't get enough of your taste on my tongue."

He prowled back up her body, his thick erection lying against her thigh. She tried to wrap her arms around his broad shoulders and winced in pain as she moved her wrist at that angle. The painkillers from last night had long worn off.

"Shit, are you okay?" he asked, immediately easing off of her. "Did I hurt you?"

"No, my arm is just a little sore. It didn't hurt until I tried to move it just now."

Mike jumped up from the bed, unabashed in his nakedness. His erection stood loud and proud, but he strode to the bathroom and was instantly back with medicine and a cup of water. "Here, drink this. I'll make us breakfast while it kicks in."

She glanced down at him. "But…."

"Honey, I'm always hard around you. Get used to it." He winked and slipped on some boxer briefs, walking out of the master bedroom.

Kenley heard him rummaging around in the kitchen, along with the clanking of pots and pans. She should offer to help him, but how much use would she really be with her injured wrist? Plus the painkillers would take a little while to start working. She snuggled back under the covers and shut her eyes. Maybe if she drifted off to sleep for a few minutes, she'd feel better.

***

"Do you have to go into work today?" Mike asked as he set a steaming plate of bacon, eggs, toast, and chocolate chip pancakes in front of her. Kenley looked thoroughly sated, he thought smugly. Her face was flushed, her eyes glowing, and that gorgeous head of curls was rumpled like she'd spent the entire night rolling around between the sheets. Which they pretty much had.

"Wow, this looks delicious, but I'll never be able to eat all this."

Mike shrugged. "I wasn't sure what you liked."

"Well, thanks. I'm starving."

Mike grinned. "I wonder why you've got such an appetite this morning," he teased. Kenley turned an even rosier hue but smiled at him.

"No idea," she commented dryly. "And to answer your question, my boss left me a message this morning, telling me to take the day off. Someone else is driving all that paperwork for the new hires down, and HR from the home office will schedule the second round of interviews. I'll be the one conducting them of course, which means I'll be back at it tomorrow. But at least I have a day to take it easy."

Mike frowned. After the night she'd been through, one day hardly seemed like enough recovery time. And he hadn't exactly let her get a ton of rest last night, he thought guiltily.

"What time is it? Don't you guys usually go in really early? I thought Christopher always had to be on base at the crack of dawn."

"That we do," Mike agreed. "We've got a later start time today though because we'll be doing some night training."

"Oh, with night vision goggles and stuff? Are you going to deploy soon?"

"Don't know. We don't get much advance notice. When you're a SEAL, you're pretty much at Uncle

Sam's beck and call twenty-four seven. We can be ready to roll out in a matter of hours."

Kenley frowned, and Mike felt a wave of uneasiness wash over him. Was she concerned about his missions or the fact that he was gone a lot of the time? He didn't like the idea of her being upset or worried about him. Usually when his SEAL team was sent on an op, he didn't worry about a thing back at home. If the idea of leaving Kenley behind gave him second thoughts about leaving, then what was she thinking or feeling? If things progressed between them, they'd have to discuss it at some point.

It was difficult maintaining a relationship when you were in the military, and especially when you were a SEAL. Lots of wives and girlfriends couldn't handle the stress of not knowing where the men were going, where they'd be while they were gone, or when they'd return. Not that he and Kenley were a couple or something. They'd spent one night together. A fantastic, amazing night that he was looking to repeat as soon as possible.

Mike cleared his throat. "I wish I could stop by tonight to check on you, but we'll be out late."

"Oh, it's okay," she replied, looking surprised that he wanted to check in on her. Hell, after the night they'd spent together, was it really that shocking? He cared about her. Couldn't she see that? "I'll probably just rest today and then get back to work tomorrow. That reminds me, did Matthew and Christopher have trouble with the car door? I couldn't get it open last night when I ran off the road."

"They didn't mention it. It was probably just blocked by whatever you hit. We had it towed back onto the highway, and the guys drove it back without incident. We can check it out this morning before you go if you're concerned. Or take it in to be fixed if need be."

Kenley looked slightly uncomfortable. "I can take it by a repair shop. I might need to get a recommendation from you though. My mechanic is back in Arlington, so I don't exactly know what's around here. But I need to be able to get in and out of the car."

"I'll go in with you this morning if you're worried," Mike said. "I don't have to be on base until noon."

"No, don't worry about it." She pushed the food around on her plate, and a pit settled in Mike's gut. After the past twelve hours they'd spent together, why was she pushing him away now? It was almost like she didn't want his help.

He raised his eyebrows when she looked up and met his gaze. "Thanks for offering," she hastily added. "I'm just used to doing things by myself."

"You don't have to as long as I'm here."

She shrugged. "But that's just the thing. I'll be leaving after I conduct this second round of interviews. Going back to Northern Virginia. I mean, I appreciate you offering to help me today. Let's just not pretend this is something it's not."

"Arlington's not that far away. What, maybe four hours? You think just because you're going back there that I don't want to see you again?"

"Maybe it's not too far from Virginia Beach, but it's a hell of a long way from Afghanistan."

Mike raised his eyebrows.

"Mike, I work for a Defense contractor. Maybe you can't tell me exactly where you go all the time on your deployments with the SEALs, but I certainly have an idea. When I was kid, my parents were gone all the time. I was *always* left to fend for myself, and I'm not going to do that anymore. Not in a relationship. When I do eventually meet someone," she quickly added, heat rising in her cheeks, "I want it to be someone who's there for me."

Mike's gut twisted. It was true, when out on deployments, he wouldn't physically be there. And he might not readily be able to contact her at every moment. But hell, Mike would do whatever was in his power to make sure Kenley always felt safe and secure. Hadn't he driven out in the rainstorm last night looking for her after she called? Hadn't his friend hacked into the cell networks to pinpoint her exact location? And hell, lots of couples had long distance relationships. Maybe that wouldn't work for an entire lifetime, but was she really not willing to give him a shot at all?

It figured. After all the women chasing after him over the years, the one who'd caught his attention was also the one who wanted to slip away. The hell with this.

"So we spend one spectacular night together, and that's it?"

"What do you want me to say?"

"Say you felt what I did," he said, rising from his chair and kneeling down in front of her. They were exactly at eye level now, and he nailed her with a gaze.

"Mike...."

She looked so lost, he wanted to envelop her in his arms. Promise her that he would be there for her. "You didn't feel anything?" he asked, leaning in slightly closer as her breath hitched. "Not even when you came on my fingers or my tongue? When my cock was buried so deep inside you and you screamed out my name?"

Her lower lip trembled. Hell. He wasn't trying to make her cry, just to make her admit that she felt something for him, too. That they weren't just some one-night-stand.

"If I kissed you right now, you're saying it wouldn't mean anything to you?"

"Don't make this harder than it is," she pleaded.

He lifted a hand to her face, and his thumb skimmed over her lower lip. He leaned in slowly, ready to kiss her sweet lips once more.

"Stop," she said, pushing her good hand against his chest. "Just stop."

Mike froze, his chest tightening.

"I should go," she whispered, scooting her chair back and rising.

"Kenley—"

"I have to go!"

"Let me get your things," Mike conceded, rising to help her. She didn't have much—just her purse and the clothes she'd been wearing last night. She couldn't exactly go home in her cut up blouse. Kenley seemed to realize the same thing and glanced down at the shirt she had on—one of Mike's tee shirts. "You keep it. You need something to wear home."

She nodded uncertainly, tears welling in her eyes. He'd let her go now. She was spooked. Scared. But that sure the hell didn't mean he was willing to let her walk out of his life for good. Not when she just may be the best damn thing that had ever happened to him.

Chapter 15

Kenley glanced around the coffee shop from a table in the back an hour later, inhaling the scent of freshly roasted beans. There weren't many people here this morning—many of the tourists had gone home after the weekend, and the locals were at work. There were some cute grandmotherly types seated a couple of tables over and a young couple, but she and Lexi mostly had the place to themselves.

Kenley wrapped her sweater around her shoulders, chilled despite the hot drink she was sipping. Her whole world felt off-kilter after the past twenty-four hours, and settling in with her best friend for some girl talk was exactly what she needed.

"Wait, so what happened?" Lexi asked, confusion clouding her face.

"I left," Kenley answered simply.

"You left him right there in his kitchen?"

"Well what was I supposed to do? We spent a

night together. Mike seemed to think that meant we should start a long distance relationship or something. I mean we barely even know each other! We've never gone out on a date. We've never spent a day together just hanging out, seeing what we have in common. Yes, he helped me, and I'll be forever grateful for that. But that doesn't mean we're a couple now."

"He was really worried about you," Lexi protested. "Christopher had him on speaker phone when we were trying to locate you, and that man was in a near panic."

"He was worried, I know. I get that he's a decent guy most of the time. I mean he's still a bit too cocky for my taste, but he can be sweet."

"So what's the problem?"

"He's the kind of guy that *always* has a woman around. I saw him at the bonfire; I've heard stories about all the guys on the SEAL team. I'm not anything special to him."

Lexi's eyes softened. "Sweetie, of course you're special."

Kenley rolled her eyes. "I don't need you to patronize me. I'm not anything special to him. Mike's the kind of guy that's been with dozens of women. Trust me when I say he knows his way around a woman's body—holy hell."

Lexi laughed. "Whoa, slow down. What exactly happened last night after he found you?"

Kenley leaned in closer, whispering a few of the details so that the other patrons in the coffee shop didn't hear them. Because that was all she needed, somebody's grandma knowing all about her sex life. She took a sip of her café mocha as Lexi's eyes grew wider and wider.

"Well, we can't say he isn't thorough," Lexi teased.

Kenley nearly spit out her coffee. "Shhh!"

Lexi laughed. "And you're willing to give up all that just because you think he wouldn't be willing to give up the single life for you? Because you're going home in a week or two? He wouldn't suggest seeing you again if he didn't mean it."

"It's not just that," Kenley admitted. "Even if, say, something did start up between us…."

"I'd say it already has."

Kenley glared at her best friend. "The point is, Mike wouldn't be around. I dealt with that all the time growing up, and I just don't want that for my future. What if we had kids? Then their dad would just be gone half the time? I lived that life, and it sucked."

Lexi raised her eyebrows. "So you've considered having kids with the man, but you won't date him. Interesting."

Kenley blew out an exasperated sigh. "You know what I mean."

"Don't you think you're putting the cart before the horse? Maybe the long distance thing won't work for you. Maybe you'll meet someone else. Maybe the whole thing will fizzle out in a month or two. But don't give up on your entire future without even giving him a shot."

"You seem pretty confident."

"Kenley, I've never seen you look at a man the way you do Mike. Ever. And the way he rushed off to find you like that in the middle of the rainstorm? That man cares about you. So what if he's been with a hundred women in the past. I assure you he doesn't bring them home with him. Or cook them breakfast in the morning. Or, what, offer to get your car fixed for you? Guys just don't do that for women they have no interest in."

"I don't know...."

"Hey, he already slept with you. Multiple times from the sounds of it."

"Lexi!" Kenley hissed.

She laughed and took a sip of her latte. "I'm just saying, he wasn't doing all that to get you into bed. He already had, you know? He cares about you."

"We barely know each other," Kenley muttered.

Lexi shrugged. "You guys have chemistry. A connection. You can't fake that, and you can't fight it either. And even if you claim you'll never see him again, that's not going to happen. Christopher and I will be planning our wedding. You'll have to see Mike at some point. And do you really want him bringing some other woman along as his date?"

Kenley's stomach dropped at that image. No, she didn't want Mike kissing, dating, or sleeping with any other women. But that didn't mean she was ready to fall head-over-heels for him either.

***

Mike cursed as he pulled onto base just before noon. Christopher was getting out of his pickup truck a few spots down, which meant Mike would have to deal with another round of twenty questions. Fucking perfect. After the way Kenley had blown him off this morning, he wasn't in the mood to talk to anyone. Hell, the very first time he'd cared about a woman enough to bring her home, she up and bails on him at breakfast? Weren't women supposed to like that sort of thing? Usually Mike was the one running out the door the morning after, offering his excuses. It twisted his gut to be on the receiving end of that kind of brush-off.

"It's gonna be a long day, man," Christopher said, slinging his duffle bag over his shoulder. "I'm psyched for some night ops training though."

"No kidding," Mike grumbled.

"So is Kenley doing okay after the accident? Lexi left earlier to meet her at a coffee shop. I figured she'd be spending the whole morning with you."

"So did I," Mike said as they fell in step beside one another. "Kenley didn't exactly like my suggestion of seeing each other when she went back to Arlington. You'd think most women would be thrilled a guy didn't want to blow them off after one night."

Christopher chuckled. "Maybe she doesn't want to do the long distance thing?"

"That's part of it. I don't think she likes the military thing either."

"But she stayed at your place last night?"

"Yep."

Christopher raised his eyebrows expectantly.

"Not gonna lie, man, it was pretty fucking spectacular. Not enough to convince her to give it a go another time though. Hell, I've never even taken her out on a date. We've been together in all these group situations—the bonfire, the pool. And without going into details, let's just say the chemistry between us is off the charts."

"So ask her out. On a real date—dinner, flowers, the works."

"Pretty sure she'd turn me down, man," Mike said.

"She still arguing with you half the time?"

"Not last night, no. That was the first time she let

her guard down and I got to see the real Kenley."

"Foreplay, man."

"What?"

"All that fighting you were doing was nothing but foreplay. No wonder last night was so spectacular. Trust me, after ten years of Lexi being angry with me, when we reconnected this summer? Fucking amazing."

Mike laughed. Christopher and Lexi were hardly the same as him and Kenley. They had a history together. He'd had but a few encounters over the past month with the woman he was falling for. Yes, he wanted more—much more. But if the woman wouldn't give him a damn chance....

Patrick nodded at them in greeting as they walked into the locker room. "What's fucking amazing?"

"Just the woman of his dreams," Christopher snickered.

"Kenley bailed on me this morning," Mike said, stuffing his gear into his locker. "As in she couldn't get out of my place fast enough."

"So she spent the night."

"Yeah. She doesn't like that I'm a SEAL though. Or that we live four hours apart."

"You're not going to be a SEAL forever," Patrick pointed out. "None of us will. And hell, who knows what'll happen next month or next year?"

"That's true enough," Christopher agreed. "If she works up in Arlington, and things did somehow work out for you, you could get a job at the Pentagon."

"Somehow work out?" Mike mumbled. "Hell, things barely even got started."

"You could find her again in ten years like Christopher did with Lexi," Patrick said with a smirk.

"Best thing to ever happen to me," Christopher admitted. "I wouldn't suggest waiting ten years to chase after her though."

Mike blew out a breath, slamming his locker shut as the men headed to the weight room for some PT. "Maybe I don't want what you guys have. I'm doing just fine on my own."

"Right," Patrick chuckled. "Then why the hell do you look so damn miserable?"

Chapter 16

Kenley stood outside her favorite bar in DC two weeks later, waiting for Lexi. She tapped her foot impatiently as she watched the masses leaving work. Men in business suits, men in khakis and polo shirts all streamed by. They were attractive, yes, but not one of them caught her interest the way that Mike had.

She'd been back for only a few days, her assignment down in Norfolk complete. She hadn't seen Mike once during her remainder of time there. He'd texted her the day after their argument to make sure she was okay, but after the brief message she'd sent him back, she hadn't heard from him since. Not that she expected to. He probably wasn't used to women blowing him off. Besides, those guys had a parade of women around them all the time. The second she'd walked out his door he was probably already moving on to the next willing and available female.

Ugh, she thought with a groan. If only the sex hadn't been so off-the-charts spectacular. Then maybe she could move on with her plan of finding a stable guy to settle down with. Memories of Mike's hard body moving over hers were giving her little incentive to find a "safe" guy though. She doubted anyone would ever get her as worked up as him. She almost wished she'd returned to his apartment before she left for one last night together. Her face flamed just thinking about it.

Jesus, he'd seemed to get just as turned on as her by making her come over and over in his bed. Other guys were more about seeking their own pleasure. But with Mike? She'd felt like a goddess he was worshipping. And who wouldn't want to be basking in all that attention of a sexy Navy SEAL?

They argued half of the time they'd been around each other though. Maybe not that last night, but it's not like they'd gotten off to the best start. Which only further confirmed that things between them would never work. Maybe the distance wasn't as big a deal as she claimed—it wouldn't be forever. After all, Lexi was moving down to Virginia Beach to be with her man. That type of life would never work for her though.

"Kenley!" Lexi called out, rushing down the block. Her jet black hair swished around the sleek suit she was wearing, and not a few pairs of male eyes slid her way. Of course. She was stunning and beautiful. Kenley was more petite and cute—but not exactly the type of women men chased down the street after. Not that Mike had been complaining.

"Hey! You made it," Kenley said. "I'm in desperate need of a martini."

"Me too. The first week back after my month off is killing me. I didn't think I'd be so tired after only a couple of days."

Kenley dragged Lexi inside, and they fought their way through the happy hour crowd to snag some space at the bar. A young bartender approached, and they each ordered drinks. The bartender's gaze quickly swept over Kenley, taking in the deep v-neck of the navy blue wrap dress she had on. Without the blazer she'd worn to work covering her, her ample cleavage was on display. She warmed slightly at his appreciative glance but found herself strangely wishing Mike could see her in it instead.

Not that she planned to see him again. Ever.

"Any word on the new job?" Kenley asked, stirring the olive around in the martini the bartender placed in front of her. Holy crap. Had he written his phone number on the napkin?

Lexi caught sight of it too and giggled. "Picking up men in crowded bars? Mike wouldn't be too happy about that," she teased.

Kenley flushed. "Mike can date whoever he wants, and so can I."

Lexi raised her eyebrows. She took a sip of her Merlot and watched Kenley, waiting expectantly.

"Okay, so I don't plan to actually *call* the bartender. Please. But that doesn't mean anything."

Lexi shrugged. "Sure. And as for the new job, not yet, but you know how the government works—at a snail's pace."

Kenley eyed her best friend suspiciously. Why was she bringing up Mike tonight anyway? They hadn't even talked about him once since the coffee shop a couple of weeks ago—Kenley had made it very clear that that conversation was over. For good.

"And you're doing okay on your own?" she asked, changing the subject. "You're still more than welcome to stay at my place if you want."

"I'm fine. It's strange, but being back home, I don't have as many fears."

"It makes sense. You're back where you're comfortable."

"Speaking of comfortable, I just noticed your cast is gone!"

"Just got it off this morning," Kenley said, grinning. "I can't say I miss it."

"Yeah, I bet that's a relief. So did your parents ever get back from that cruise?"

"Not yet. It's a month long. I did finally reach them via email, and get this, all my mom said was 'Glad you're okay, sweetie.' You'd think running off the road and breaking my wrist would've justified a phone call or something."

"I'm sorry, hun. I don't think they're ever going to change."

Kenley shrugged. "It's fine. I'm used to it by now. I mean they supported me financially when I was younger, they just weren't ever around."

"That sucks, sweetie."

"Yep." She drained the rest of her martini. No sense in lingering on the past now. She hadn't exactly had a bad childhood, just absentee parents. There was always food on the table, a warm place to live, a nanny to take care of her and her sister.

"Oh!" Lexi gasped, glancing toward the bar entrance.

"What?" Kenley asked, swiveling around on her barstool. Only one thing could light up her best friend's face like that, but the chances of Christopher walking through the door were slim to none. Her stomach dropped when she caught sight of Mike standing beside Lexi's fiancé. He cleaned up nicely, in khaki pants and a button down shirt. It did little to conceal the pounds of muscle that lay beneath, and he scanned the room, his chiseled features drawing the attention of many of the women.

His blue gaze locked with hers, and her heart pounded furiously in her chest. He'd come for her. Driven all the way up here to…what? Talk? Ask her on a proper date? Drag her off to bed? She flushed as he took a step closer. The way his gaze ran over her torso felt like a caress. Shakily, she stood up as Lexi whispered that she'd pay for their round of drinks. Christopher was already moving toward Lexi, but Kenley brushed past him, hurrying toward Mike, who was rooted by the door.

***

Kenley walked toward him, face flushed, curls bouncing around her head, and that sexy-as-fuck dress clinging to her like a second skin. The way it wrapped around her breasts should be illegal—he'd have to convince her not to wear things like that when he wasn't around. Because hell, the things he wanted to do to her…she was like a present, just waiting for him to unwrap. The dark blue set off her ivory skin, and for a moment, he was again reminded of a painting. She looked like a goddess stepping out of a canvas, headed straight for him.

She stopped in front of him, not hesitating to meet his gaze. Her heels made her a bit taller, but she still only reached his shoulder. His eyes were drawn to her chest rapidly rising and falling. Was she angry? Aroused? In complete shock to see him?

"Your cast is off," he finally said, his voice sounding gruffer than expected.

She swallowed. "I just got it off this morning."

"So you're okay?"

"Fine," she said, her voice wavering. "Fine," she repeated.

Unable to help himself, he reached out, brushing one of those curls back from her face, his hand skimming across her cheek. She looked so fragile and delicate, he wanted to tuck her against him, hold her close, and keep her safe. Forever.

Hell. He'd never had any such desires with a woman before. But something about her made him want to protect and honor her. Cherish her. Love her.

"You left without saying goodbye," he said quietly.

"You knew I was leaving."

He nodded. "That doesn't mean I like the idea of you walking right out of my life. Hell, Kenley, I've never taken a woman home before. Never made her breakfast, offered to help her fix her car. I care about you."

Her mouth dropped open in surprise. "But you guys always have women hanging around—I'm not stupid. I'm not blind. Why me?"

"Because you're the only woman I've had to chase after. You're not afraid to talk back to me, to tell me like it is. To call me out when I'm being an asshole. You rushed down to help your best friend when she needed you. And because you're the prettiest woman I've ever seen."

"Mike…." Her voice sounded breathless. His heart

pounded furiously in his chest. Damn, it felt like a herd of galloping horses. He jumped out of airplanes, fought with unknown enemies, shot at insurgents. And he couldn't tell a woman how he felt without his nerves getting in the way?

"I'm scared of the way I feel around you," she admitted. "I do like you—even if you can be arrogant some of the time, you're a good guy. But I just feel so out of control when we're together."

His hands slid to her waist, pulling her closer toward him.

"I feel completely out of control when I'm with you," he said huskily.

He cupped her chin, tilting it up. Her vanilla scent washed over him, and his groin tightened. Kenley was so damn sweet it almost hurt just to look at her. He ducked lower and kissed her softly, gently. Promising her everything that was to come.

Her hands slid around his neck, and those tempting breasts pushed against his chest. Damn. She was so soft and yielding to him, just completely perfect. "Take me home," he instructed, breaking their kiss. "Let me make love to you all night."

"But how did you manage to get leave?" she asked. "I thought you had to be on call twenty-four seven."

Mike shrugged, a smile tugging at his lips. "Christopher assured our CO that it was urgent. I've only got the night, and then I have to drive back. We've got late training again tomorrow. Lexi said you two could come down this weekend though."

Kenley raised her eyebrows.

"Surprise," Mike said.

Kenley laughed, and then looked back toward the bar. Mike's gaze followed hers.

Christopher had his arms wrapped around Lexi, and she waved at Mike and Kenley from across the room. He'd have to thank both of them later on for convincing him to go after Kenley.

Her small hand slipped into his, and he glanced down. "Let's go," she said.

"Where are you taking me?"

"My place. And you're not allowed to leave until morning."

Chapter 17

Kenley and Mike hurried hand-in-hand through the lobby of her apartment building. Mike's jaw was set in a firm line, his eyes dark with arousal, and there was no mistaking the bulge that had formed in his pants. The metro ride back to Arlington from DC had been torture, with Mike whispering suggestively in her ear the entire time. By the time they'd reached the station, she was all but ready to rip her dress off right then and there.

The cool October evening did little to chill her overheated flesh as they'd rushed down the block to her apartment. She had a feeling that if Mike had known the way, he'd have scooped her up and carried her there himself in an effort to make haste. Not that that would have drawn attention to them or anything, she'd thought with a smirk.

The elevator doors finally opened, and Mike backed her against the wall as they rode up to her floor, his spicy scent making her dizzy with desire. His hands rested on the wall on either side of her head, his muscular arms caging her in as he bent over. He was big and strong and looked ready to completely devour her. But despite his aggressive stance, he kissed her softly, his mouth moving slowly against hers, holding back.

The elevator dinged as it finally reached her floor, and she practically dragged Mike down the hallway. The second her apartment door swung shut behind her, Mike was on her, kissing her passionately. "It's been too long since I've touched you," he growled, backing her against the door until his hard body was pressed against hers.

She felt every inch of him, from his broad pecs and solid abs to his thick arousal. She trembled as his lips skimmed down the column of her neck, his breath hot on her flesh, his teeth grazing her sensitive skin. His hands fumbled with the sash at her waist, tugging it until her dress fell open.

Hot hands brushed over her skin. Her breasts swelled and nipples tightened as arousal dampened her panties. Mike's fingers slid across her bare shoulders, pushing the dress off, allowing the blue frock to fall to the ground. "Hey, your cast's gone," he said.

Kenley smirked. "It took you a while to notice."

Blue eyes nailed her with a gaze. In an instant, he'd captured her wrists and pinned them above her head with one hand. She gasped as he flashed her a wicked grin and then tugged one cup of her lacy bra down. He sucked one nipple into his mouth, pulling hard on the taut bud. She cried out as the feeling shot straight to her core. His tongue laved against her nipple, teasing and tormenting her, as his other hand slid to her black lace panties. She was drenched, dripping for him, and he groaned in approval as he fingered her through the delicate material.

"Fuck, Kenley, you are so wet for me." His hand slipped inside her panties, and she moaned as his fingers slid through her slick folds. Mike's breathing was heavy as he ducked his head, sucking on the skin of her neck. She didn't know who was more aroused at the moment—her or him. Two thick fingers penetrated her, and his thumb slid across her throbbing clit. She gasped and arched against him, desperate for more. Mike softly bit the tendon where her neck and shoulder met, causing her to cry out. His fingers began thrusting in and out of her core, stretching and filling her as she writhed against him. It was good, so good, but not nearly enough.

"Please," she begged. "I need you inside me."

"Not yet."

His thumb slid across her sensitive bundle of nerves, and she bucked against him. His grip tightened around her wrists as he held her in place. Molten heat slid through her veins, setting her entire body on fire. She was helpless, trapped between the door and Mike's large frame, and she'd never been so aroused in her life. He was once again in complete control, commanding her body, and she was desperate for him to bring her to release.

She glanced down at his hand pushed inside her skimpy little panties, the sight as erotic and enticing as hell. He pumped his fingers faster, harder, edging her on. His thumb circled her clit, moving faster and faster, and suddenly she exploded, crying out as she burst into a million little pieces. Mike continued his onslaught as she bucked wildly against his hand. Finally she fell back down to Earth, gasping as she tried to regain her breath.

Mike fumbled with the clasp on her bra, and cool air rushed over her nipples. He quickly shucked off his shirt and ducked down to help her step out of her lace panties. All she had on were her heels, and Mike gripped her ankles, instructing her to leave them on. It was sexy as hell having him hold her in place like that, and her breath caught as he gazed up at her from where he knelt, his expression wild. Mike was a man on the edge, and she wanted to take him up the precipice and send him soaring.

"Just one taste," he muttered, hooking her leg over his shoulder.

She was completely bare, exposed to him, and his mouth was on her in an instant. He grabbed her hips, pulling her closer, holding her to him. He licked, sucked, and lapped at her, drinking in all of her juices. Long swipes of his tongue were interspersed with tiny ministrations, and she was whimpering within moments. Teasing her swollen clit, he brought her higher once more. She grabbed onto his head, her fingernails scraping against his scalp as he devoured her. Her legs began trembling, and a moment later, Mike had lifted her other leg onto his shoulder, so she was leaning against the door, legs spread wide over his broad shoulders.

He slid two fingers inside her tight channel once more, and she exploded, bucking against his mouth as he suckled her clit. Finally Mike lifted her off him but stood, holding her steady as if she weighed nothing at all. He backed her against the door, lining his throbbing erection up with her wet heat. "I've wanted to do this since the first day I met you," he confessed as he slowly pushed inside.

She gasped, clinging to his broad shoulders. He was so big, bigger than she remembered, his cock like velvet-covered steel. He was so hot and hard for her, she eagerly took him in, the aftershocks from her orgasm causing her walls to continuously spasm, until he filled her completely. Mike inside of her felt like coming home—like she'd been missing something all along without ever knowing it. She'd never tire of the feel of this man inside her, joined with her. It was just about the closest thing to heaven she'd ever known.

Mike gently began thrusting, gripping her ass with muscular hands, forcing her to ride up and down his shaft. She cried out as waves of pleasure began to overtake her once more. She'd barely come down from her last high and Mike was already building her up.

She couldn't control anything in this position, she was simply at Mike's complete mercy as he claimed her. He stepped away from the door so she was solely supported by him, completely impaled by his erection. She cried out again and again as he thrust deeply. Gasping, she threw her head back. His mouth captured one breast, and he sucked eagerly, bucking into her, until she was crying out his name in ecstasy.

"Oh my God," she gasped as she finally collapsed against him.

"Bedroom," he demanded.

"Down the hall," she murmured, her lips brushing against his neck. He smelled so good, like man and spice and comfort. Like home. Maybe her own parents hadn't been there for her, but Mike had proven that he would be.

He carried her down the hall, still buried deep inside her. It was erotic as hell having him hold her this way, their bodies still joined. She never wanted it to end.

Mike sat on the edge of the bed as she straddled him, and her eyes grew wide as he hardened once more.

Mike shot her a cocky grin. "I told you, I'm always hard around you."

"Jesus. I'm never going to get any rest with you around."

He raised one eyebrow. "Is that a bad thing?"

"Not at all," she said, kissing him passionately.

"So about this weekend," he interrupted, breaking off their kiss.

"I'll be there," she promised.

"So we're giving this a go between us?"

"Absolutely. I want this to work. And if we have to do the long-distance thing for a while, then we'll do it. I've never felt the way that I do when we're together."

"I'm falling in love with you Kenley," he said, meeting her eyes.

She happily sighed. "I think I've already fallen in love with you."

Epilogue

Kenley giggled a month later as Mike pulled her into his lap at a seafood restaurant down by the ocean. She hastily set her drink down, not wanting to spill red wine all over herself, as Mike's muscular arms wrapped around her, holding her tight.

"I propose a toast," Lexi said, grinning.

"To what?" Kenley asked.

"To happy couples," Lexi said.

"To nights to remember," Mike added.

He drew Kenley in for a kiss as Lexi laughed and Christopher shot them a knowing grin. "Maybe we should plan a double wedding," he joked.

"You don't have to convince me," Mike teased. "It's Kenley who won't let me seal the deal."

Kenley playfully swatted his arm. "We've only been officially dating for a month. Those two have known each other ten years. I mean technically, it took Christopher that long to propose."

"Hey," he protested.

"That doesn't count," Lexi chimed in.

"So what if he did?" Mike asked. "A man can't know what he wants? I know a good thing when I see it."

"He does sound rather convincing," Lexi agreed, her violet eyes twinkling.

"Hang on a second, babe," Mike said, setting Kenley back in her chair. "I forgot something."

Kenley raised her eyebrows as Mike stood up and then quickly bent down on one knee, producing a velvet box. She gasped, raising her hands to her face in surprise, as Christopher and Lexi grinned at them.

"You knew about this!" Kenley said. "Both of you!"

Mike raised his eyebrows, waiting for her to calm down. He popped open the lid, and a beautiful diamond solitaire peeked out, nearly stealing her breath. The way her heart pounded furiously had to be from the second glass of wine she'd just enjoyed. Not from the man of her dreams down on one knee proposing.

"Kenley, I knew from the moment that we first met that I wanted you. I just didn't know how much. You make me the happiest I've ever been, and the only thing that could make me even happier is knowing that you'll be my wife. Marry me, and I'll spend the rest of my life cherishing, honoring, and protecting you."

"Are you serious?" Kenley asked, tears welling in her eyes. "You really want us to get married?"

Mike swiped a tear from her cheek, sending her an easy smile. "I've never been more sure of anything in my life. Will you marry me?"

"Yes," she whispered, tears streaming down her cheeks.

Mike leaned in closer, pulling her to him. "Baby, don't cry," he murmured softly.

"I can't help it," she said, brushing away her tears. "I'm just so happy."

Mike slipped the ring on her finger as the other couples around them clapped and cheered, the loudest of all Lexi and Christopher.

Kenley flushed at the attention and looked deep into Mike's eyes. "I love you."

"I love you, too."

They happily kissed, content to start their own perfect version of forever.

About the Author

USA Today Bestselling Author Makenna Jameison writes sizzling romantic suspense, including the addictive Alpha SEALs series. Makenna loves the beach, strong coffee, red wine, and traveling. She lives in Washington DC with her husband and two daughters.

Visit www.makennajameison.com to discover your next great read.

Want to read more from MAKENNA JAMEISON?

Keep reading for an exclusive excerpt from the fifth book in her Alpha SEALs series, *THE SEAL NEXT DOOR.*

Brianna Miller's life is in complete chaos. She's moonlighting as a cocktail waitress after getting laid off, her older brother was seriously injured in Afghanistan, and the man she's pined for since she was a teenager is back in her life, hotter than hell and more tempting than ever.

Navy SEAL Matthew "Gator" Murphy has only one goal when he returns to Pensacola, Florida for a long weekend—to welcome his best friend home and then get the hell out of there. There's no way he can face his buddy's injuries, not when he was the one who convinced him to enlist in the Navy in the first place.

When a gorgeous blonde waitress catches his eye, the last woman he expects to see is Brianna, his best friend's younger sister. The chemistry between them sizzles as Matthew tries to stay away from temptation, but sometimes a raging inferno begins with only a spark.

Chapter 1

Matthew "Gator" Murphy breathed in the humid Florida air as he strode down the ramp of the C-17 military cargo plane, duffle bag gripped tightly in his right hand. His muscles flexed with the movement, and he ground his jaw as the bright sunlight blinded him. He ran his hand through his dark, short cropped hair, instinctively realizing his helmet was missing. Scratch that. He sure the hell didn't need it here on U.S. soil. Slipping on his aviators, he walked across the tarmac on Pensacola Naval Base like he owned the place. You'd been on one military base, you'd been on them all. And with his current frame of mind, he didn't give a damn what Commanders or Admirals were wandering around. He was in a mood to kick ass and take names.

The dampness in the air clung to his skin, making him feel like he'd walked out of the climate controlled interior of the plane and straight into a sauna. The gentle breeze blowing in from the Gulf did little to cool down the air temperature—or his current mood. A few palm trees swayed in the distance next to the administration building, but the rest of the place was standard military: miles of concrete, men and women in uniform, rows upon rows of planes. He felt strange walking around in civilian gear, but for once, he wasn't hopping a ride on a transport to head overseas on an op. Most of his SEAL team buddies were back where he'd left them in Little Creek. His gear was stashed away at his apartment in Virginia.

Home sweet home was his final destination today.

"Sir," a junior officer said as he passed, saluting him.

Matthew saluted in return, a feeling of pride surging through him, temporarily replacing his anger. Even without his uniform on, he commanded attention. At 6'4" with the brawny build of a SEAL, he was used to the stares of civilians. But hell if it didn't feel good to have others in the military show him the respect he'd earned. The acknowledgement he deserved. At thirty, he'd devoted twelve years of his life to the U.S. Navy. And when a junior officer noticed his seniority, despite his lack of uniform, well didn't that feel fucking nice.

"Do you know where I can find Colton Ferguson?" Matthew asked the junior officer.

"Yes, sir. He's inside the admin building over there. Second office on the left."

"Thank you." Matthew nodded and continued on his way.

Any other time he might have welcomed the brief respite from his duties as a SEAL stationed in Little Creek, Virginia. Part of an elite six-member team that was frequently deployed on missions all over the globe, he worked hard and played harder. Drilled on the water, did daily PT with his men, trained even in his off hours, and chased after the pretty girls on the weekend. And hell. Who wouldn't enjoy a weekend back at home? A few days on the Gulf, down by the beach, far away from work?

Except the emergency leave granted so that he could attend his best friend's homecoming from Walter Reed Medical Center wasn't exactly part of the plan. Not this weekend. Not fucking ever. Best friends since childhood, Beckett Miller had been like the brother he never had. With Beckett's younger sister Brianna trailing after them, the three of them had enjoyed childhood adventures traipsing around the marshland, taking their small boat out on the water, and sneaking off to the beach after dark. Beckett had enlisted in the Navy right out of high school just like Matthew. Although Beckett was also a SEAL, he was based out of Coronado. An ambush late one night on a highway in the remote part of Afghanistan, serving his duty to Uncle Sam, had left his friend comatose for more than a month and missing one leg.

Hell. What was he supposed to say to Beckett's parents? To Beckett himself? To Beckett's sister? He hadn't even seen Brianna in years. Maybe they'd been inseparable in childhood, but today he wouldn't know the woman if she smacked right into him. Matthew had enlisted in the Navy at age eighteen. Between BUD/S out in Coronado, missions all over the world, and his current station near Virginia Beach, he had little time to spend at home. He couldn't even recall the exact date he'd last been back.

Four years his and Beckett's junior, Brianna had just been starting high school when he'd left. Then she'd gone off to college, started her own career, and the years had slipped away. He thought he remembered Beckett saying she was back in Florida, working on some type of marketing gig. Temporarily living with her parents again.

Damn.

Seeing Beckett's family would just bring up more memories of their childhood. Of a time when Beckett wasn't injured and the world was theirs to conquer and explore. With the way Matthew's gut was currently churning, he didn't think he could deal with the onslaught of memories about the life that once was. Of the future his best friend now faced. No more active duty. No more life as a SEAL. Beckett could find a desk job, sure, but guys like them were meant to be in the thick of it. To jump out of airplanes, dive in the ocean, tote around weapons, battle foreign adversaries. To see action. To camp out in the desert and haul around eighty-pounds of gear on their backs.

But with one leg? Even though Beckett could lead a normal civilian life from here on out, life as he knew it with the SEALs was over.

Fucking hell.

Matthew needed to get through this weekend and move on. Get back to life in Little Creek and his men. His missions. Tuck the pain and grief of nearly losing his best friend so far away that it never saw the light of day again. Seeing Beckett was going to be gut-wrenching. Seeing Beckett's parents and sister would be worse. Matthew was a SEAL that had survived countless missions with barely a scrape. Who had convinced his best friend to enlist in the Navy right along beside him. How was he supposed to look them in the eye knowing he had what Beckett never would again? A long career in the military, all his limbs, a normal civilian life once he eventually retired.

The guilt was nearly eating him alive.

And seeing Brianna again after all these years?

Hell.

The little girl in pigtails he'd palled around with as a kid was long gone. She was barely a teenager when he'd enlisted in the Navy. And although he hadn't missed those puppy dog eyes she'd cast upon him every now and then as they'd grown older, he was a red-blooded American male, interested in the older college girls. The co-eds with womanly figures, plenty of tempting curves, and legs that went on for miles. Not some scrawny young girl who'd been almost like a sister to him. Who he'd never see as anything other than the girl next door.

What would it be like facing her now all these years later? He felt like he'd let her down as much as anyone—convincing her brother to join the Navy. Become a SEAL. Lose a leg and nearly die.

Sweat broke out across his brow as the guilt once again churned in his stomach.

"Yo, Gator, wait up!" Evan "Flip" Jenkins, one of the men on his SEAL team, called out from behind. "Gator" was the nickname Matthew had earned back in BUD/S since he was from Florida. It was kind of ironic now since he hardly ever set foot in the state, but the name had stuck throughout his years in the Navy.

He glanced back to see Evan jogging up behind him, his short blond hair reflecting the bright sunlight. Evan tucked his phone back into his cargo pants.

"Flip, what's up?" Matthew asked.

"What time's Beckett flying in from Walter Reed?"

"Sunday at three. Why? Is the CO already expecting us back?"

"Nah, nothing like that. Some of the other guys may come down for it."

Matthew paused. The men on his team were a close-knit group, more like blood brothers than comrades. They had each other's backs both on and off the battlefield and could practically move as one unit, training and fighting together. The only guy he'd ever been closer to was Beckett. And hell, he'd known him since they were kids. But to have his SEAL team fly down for the arrival of a wounded warrior? A fellow SEAL? That was unexpected. Not to mention damn welcome.

He'd seen more casualties in war than he ever cared to—injured soldiers, innocent civilians who'd been maimed, men killed in battle. But someone he'd known his entire life? Who he barely had a childhood memory without? That shit cut deep.

Matthew cleared his throat. "I'd really appreciate it. Beckett is like family to me. And he's a fellow SEAL."

"He's a good man," Evan agreed. "I wasn't stationed with him long, but hell, it's an honor to welcome home another SEAL. Not every man is lucky enough to come back from the warzone alive."

"Damm straight," Matthew agreed.

Evan himself had been critically injured on a mission several months ago. He'd done his time in Walter Reed and was lucky enough to be able to return to active duty. Beckett may never run ops again as a SEAL, but it was a miracle he had survived. Now if Matthew could just remember that every time he felt sorry for himself. For Beckett. For having to watch his friend go through that shit.

"Do the guys need us to make arrangements for a place for them to stay?" Matthew asked.

"Nah, they're on it. The CO can't let everyone come. Cobra's flying down tomorrow," he said, referring to Brent "Cobra" Rollins, another man on their SEAL team. "Maybe Ice," he added, referring to their team leader Patrick "Ice" Foster.

"It's good of you guys to come. Drinks are on me tomorrow night."

Evan chuffed out a laugh. "They damn well better be. Ali's giving me shit about leaving."

Matthew raised his eyebrows. The carefree nurse Evan had been dating and was now living with enjoyed laughing and joking with all the men on their SEAL team. She was always up for grabbing a beer and shooting the shit with the rest of them. Getting upset over Evan being gone didn't sound like her. Not when they deployed all the damn time anyway.

"Everything okay?" Matthew asked.

Evan cleared his throat. "Yeah, uh, we haven't really told anyone yet, but Ali's pregnant."

"Holy shit," Matthew said.

Pregnant.

Holy hell.

"Uh, congratulations?" Kids were the last thing on Matthew's mind. Not to mention girlfriends, long-term relationships, and the idea of ever settling down with one woman for life. That worked for some dudes, but as for Matthew? He'd come to terms long ago with the fact that he was better off alone.

Permanently.

Evan guffawed. "It was a surprise, but a good thing. A great thing," he added, and Matthew could hear the pride in his voice. "None of the other guys know yet," Evan continued, "so keep it on the down-low for now. I have to figure out how to break the news to them."

"Roger that," Matthew said with a grin. Hell. The other guys would likely give Evan plenty of grief. They ribbed each other like brothers, and with Evan being the youngest guy on the team, he often got the worst of it. But damn, if Evan and Ali were happy, then so was Matthew. For them at least. He wasn't gonna touch the idea of settling down with a woman or raising a family with a ten-foot pole.

"Next time you talk to Ali, give her my congratulations."

"Will do. She might kill me at the moment though with how sick she's been, but I'll tell you, that woman is over-the-moon happy."

Matthew laughed. "Hell, you and Ali will make great parents."

"I'm convinced it's a girl," Evan admitted. Matthew raised his eyebrows. "It's way too soon to tell," Evan quickly added, "but I've got a gut feeling. After all the hell I raised as a kid, I guess it serves me right. I'm going to have to worry about all the boys chasing after her when she's a teenager."

"Damn. That means I'm never, ever having a kid," Matthew muttered. "Karma's a bitch."

Evan's phone buzzed, and he held it up for Matthew to see, miming a slicing motion across his throat. Alison's name flashed across the screen.

"Let me talk to her," Matthew said. Evan

answered and then passed him the phone.

"Congratulations, darlin'," Matthew drawled.

"I'm going to kill Evan for knocking me up!" Alison wailed. "I've been sick all day long. I know that's normal—I'm a nurse for God's sake. But do I really have to survive only on saltines and ginger ale for the next nine months?"

"Aw, hell, sweetheart. That boy is practically grinning from ear-to-ear right now at the idea of being a dad. Do you need me to rough him up a little or something? Maybe if I punch him in the gut he'll get sick, too. Would that make you feel better?"

Alison weakly laughed. "Don't you dare touch him, Matthew!"

Matthew smirked. "Wouldn't dream of it. Let me put boy wonder back on."

He handed the phone back to Evan, shaking his head, and began walking toward the administration building. Evan trailed behind him, finishing up his call. A year ago every man on the team had been single. Now, save for himself and Brent, the other four guys were all playing happily ever after with their girlfriends. Un-fucking-believable. His SEAL team leader Patrick and his girlfriend Rebecca each had kids from previous relationships, but the other guys were kid-free. Now Evan and Alison were adding a baby to the mix of their group of friends?

Damn.

Life was moving on at a wicked pace without him. Before long the rest of those guys would probably be married and looking to find a less dangerous career. Not that he blamed them. Life as a SEAL made it tough to maintain any semblance of a relationship, which was part of the reason he was still single. But it worked for him. Suited him. And if he ever did happen to meet a woman he was willing to give it all up for? Well, he'd cross that bridge if and when he came to it. Which was likely not ever gonna happen.

Pushing open the heavy door to the admin building, a blast of AC rushed over his heated skin. It felt pretty damn amazing. Pushing his aviators atop his head, he strode down the hall and looked around for the office of the man he'd gone through BUD/S with years ago. Life in the military was funny sometimes, because no matter what base he was headed to, he or one of the other guys already had a contact there. Matthew had made a call to an old friend and simple as that, he had a ride home from Pensacola. They'd drop Evan off at a hotel and then Matthew would face the music, returning to his childhood home. It wasn't even his own parents he had qualms about seeing, just his buddy Beckett's. Who happened to live right next door.

Evan caught up to him in the hall. "So you went through basic with this guy Colton?"

Matthew nodded. "Affirmative. We've kept in touch over the years. He's doing a one-year tour here in Pensacola, but normally he's an explosives guy."

"Yeah. Kind of figured with the name 'C-4'," Evan laughed.

Matthew smirked and knocked on the door of the office of Colton "C-4" Ferguson, clutching his duffle bag. It probably would've been easier catching a cab—then there'd be no need to explain to his old buddy what he was doing here in Pensacola. No reminder of his wounded friend. But damn. The sooner they got this show on the road, the sooner this weekend could be over. He didn't know if he could stomach seeing his best buddy injured. And what the hell kind of a friend did that make him anyway? He should be damn glad Beckett was alive, not feeling guilty for the things he could do that his friend would never be able to again. The sooner he faced Beckett and their new reality, the sooner Matthew could move forward with his life. Pretend this shit storm never happened.

With his SEAL team he had a mission, a purpose. But back home, when his best friend would be arriving in a wheelchair, missing one limb? No matter how hard he fought, how strong he was, nothing could change the past. Nothing could erase Beckett's injury. And for the first time ever, Matthew felt completely helpless.

Now Available in Paperback!